BOOKS BY PATRICK MCGRATH

Blood and Water and Other Tales
The Grotesque
Spider

Dr. Haggard's
DISEASE

PATRICK McGRATH

POSEIDON PRESS

NEW YORK LONDON TORONTO SYDNEY TOKYO SINGAPORE

POSEIDON PRESS

Simon & Schuster Building
Rockefeller Center
1230 Avenue of the Americas
New York, New York 10020

POSEIDON PRESS is a registered trademark
of Simon & Schuster Inc.

POSEIDON PRESS colophon is a trademark
of Simon & Schuster Inc.

Designed by Karolina Harris
Manufactured in the United States of America

1   3   5   7   9   10   8   6   4   2

Library of Congress Cataloging-in-Publication Data
McGrath, Patrick. date.
Dr. Haggard's disease / Patrick McGrath.
p.   cm.
1. World War, 1939–1945 — England — Fiction.   2. Physicians — Fiction.
I. Title.   II. Title : Doctor Haggard's disease.
PS3563.C3663D7   1993
813'.54 — dc20   92-45271
CIP

ISBN: 0-671-72733-8

Acknowledgment

For the immense help he's given me—
medical, psychiatric, and literary—
not only on this book but on *Spider* as well—
I'd like to express my love and gratitude
to my father, Dr. Patrick McGrath.

For Maria

We two being one, are it.

JOHN DONNE

I WAS IN ELGIN, upstairs in my study, gazing at the sea and reflecting, I remember, on a line of Goethe when Mrs. Gregor tapped at the door that Saturday and said there was a young man to see me in the surgery, a pilot. You know how she talks. "A *pilot*, Mrs. Gregor?" I murmured. I hate being disturbed on my Saturday afternoons, especially if Spike is playing up, as he was that day, but of course I limped out onto the landing and made my way downstairs. And you know what that looks like—pathetic bloody display that is, first the good leg, then the bad leg, then the stick, good leg, bad leg, stick, but down I came, down the stairs, old beyond my years and my skin a gray so cachectic it must have suggested even to you that I was in pain, chronic pain, but oh dear boy not pain like yours, just wait now and we'll make it all—go—away—

I crossed the hall, you'd have heard the floorboards, and opened the surgery door. Always full of shadows that room, no matter how bright the day, and stinking of ether, but there on the far side, over by the cabinet, a figure. And the figure turned. And it was, indeed, a pilot, this I could now see clearly, a dark-haired young man of eighteen or nineteen in a blue uniform with wings over the left breast. You approached me rather formally and held out your hand. "Dr. Haggard?" you said.

What did I do, nod? Sigh?

"My name is James Vaughan," you said. You didn't falter. You said: "I believe you knew my mother."

Oh God. *I believe you knew my mother*—had you *any* idea the effect those words would have on me? I don't believe you did. I don't believe you did.

I closed the door and limped over to my chair. You sank gracefully into the chair on the other side of the desk and crossed your legs, and I couldn't help observing how you crossed them, in the exact same way that *she'd* always crossed her legs, with the one ankle pulled in close to the other and the foot pointing at the floor. I could hear nothing but the throbbing of blood in my head and the cry of a gull from the cliffs. As calmly as I could I offered you a cigarette but was unable to light it, for my hands were shaking. You half rose from your seat and lit both cigarettes with a small flat silver-plated lighter. "Tea?" I said.

"Lovely." You even *sounded* like her!

I went to the door, stepped into the hall and called Mrs. Gregor, who appeared from the kitchen wiping her hands on her apron, and asked her for tea. Everything seemed to be happening so slowly.

"Look, is this a bad time?" you said, suddenly suspecting that my unease was caused by your interrupting me in the middle of something important.

"Not at all," I said. "Excuse my agitation, I don't—that is, I haven't seen your mother since—"

The sentence died in the surgery's gloom. Neither of us said a word, and the uneasy fluster of the first minutes subsided as we pondered the immense unspoken world that filled the silence between us like a gas. Then our eyes met across the desk and locked for an instant, just as Mrs. Gregor turned the doorknob, pushed the door open with her bottom and backed into the surgery with the tea tray. We smiled. "I'm awfully sorry doctor," she said, "but we're out of biscuits."

"Oh dear," I said, my eyes still upon you, "I don't think we can manage without biscuits."

"There's never anything in the house on Saturdays," Mrs. Gregor remarked, setting the tray on the desk then leaving the surgery and closing the door softly behind her.

You continued smiling as I lifted the lid off the teapot and peered at the contents. That you should be *here*, her *son*, in *Elgin*—! As I poured the milk I glanced over and saw you suddenly scratch at the fabric of your trousers—the smile vanished—you frowned—and I tried to remember the last time I'd felt her presence as acutely as I felt it then.

It was at a funeral I first saw her, did she ever tell you that? And do you know, I can't remember whose it was! Who was dead, I mean. It was October 1937, a fine, crisp day, and the air in London had a sort of smoky quality to it. The leaves drifting off the chestnuts along Jubilee Road heaped themselves on the pavement and between the iron railings and crunched underfoot as I hurried along. I'd been up all night in Accident and Casualty, so I arrived ten minutes after the service began. I was wearing my black suit of course, and my black overcoat, and I slipped into the pew at the very back of the church and sat down clutching my hat (a black homburg) and adopted the sort of demeanor one does at funerals. There was a ripple of disturbance and a few heads turned, then it subsided. I'd been working at St. Basil's only six weeks or so, but I recognized a number of the doctors, including Vincent Cushing, and, in the pew in front of me, the senior pathologist. Him I knew only slightly, and I'd formed no particularly strong impression of the man. This would change, of course; as you know, your father was to have a profound impact on my life (Spike is with me still, if proof were needed) though at the time, as I sat with my homburg in my lap and gazed at the broad black back and the roll of pink flesh at the collar, I naturally had no inkling of any of this. But here's the curious thing, and I've thought about this often and I still don't know why, I'm still no closer to an explanation—what

was it that immediately riveted my attention on the woman
by his side?

Oh, I hardly need describe her to you! When I first came
into the church hers was one of the heads that turned, and I
believe that the sight of me—panting, disheveled, and late—
amused her, and so I had my first brief glimpse of her smile.
Dear James, that smile! It seemed to say that nothing should
ever dampen one's spirits not even the ghastly grim pomp of
a medical funeral! She was a tiny gamine creature all bundled
up in a big black coat with a fox round the neck and a smart
black hat with a folded-back brim. The face in the fur was
pale and heart-shaped with delicate bones and eyebrows fine
and black as pencil lines. Her eyes were startlingly clear. They
seemed to be wetly shining, somehow, and it was impossible
not to respond, and I did, I returned her smile, but was that
enough? Enough to start the germ in me? Funerals have always
affected me strongly, and this may at least partly explain it;
but to captivate me so utterly with a smile, and a smile, at
that, amid the stiff black backs of a churchful of mourners—
is the heart really so impulsive, so mercurial an organ as that?
Perhaps it is. Afterwards, when we milled around outside the
church, I lost sight of her, nor did I see her later in the
graveyard, but there was a moment when the coffin was being
borne down the aisle to the waiting hearse outside, and we
turned toward it, that I stole a glance in her direction, and
again our eyes met; and I think you might say that from that
point forward I was done for. I was lost.

Since that day I have changed in ways that I think would
astonish you. The man you know—the man I have become—
is but a phantom of the man who first glimpsed your mother
in a north London church, and caught her eye, and fell in
love—that man is dead, and in his place there's just this, oh,
this limping shadow—

Don't move, darling boy. Don't fight it.

•   •   •

So yes, I did know your mother—though when you sat there in the surgery that Saturday afternoon, and asked the question, I'm afraid I was unable to say a word—the resemblance was so uncanny! "Yes," I said at last, "I did. We knew each other well."

A pause, a hush, as you gazed at me expectantly. "I'm sorry, would you like more tea?"

"No thank you."

"We knew each other for several months," I said, "and then I moved down here, down to the sea."

Down to the sea. The lonely sea and the sky. Down to this small, forgotten sea resort, this is where I came, broken in body and spirit, to practice general medicine. Here I felt I could find peace and obscurity, here in this quiet seaside town with its esplanade and its pier, its Marine Park Gardens, with every lunchtime in the summer a performance of light symphonic music by the Municipal Orchestra. It suits me here, it's kind to broken men like me. I fell silent. Shadows deepened, evening was coming on. You wanted to know much more but you couldn't pour out your questions, you were far too reticent, or too well-mannered, for that. So you struggled to find a way, and though a few gambits suggested themselves there was, to you, something distasteful about the whole tactic, and finally you opted for plain candor. "Were you," you said, "her lover?"

Was I her lover? What was I to tell you? You were her son, after all, and I suddenly felt that the moment was one of extreme delicacy, and that what I said next would profoundly influence the nature and course of our relationship. Was I to tell you the truth, and arouse—what? The rage of the child who sees his family riven and holds the intruder to blame? But if I lied to you, or somehow blurred the outline of the thing, wouldn't that be worse? Wouldn't I then forfeit any chance I had of winning your trust? And I wanted your trust, for I wanted to hear you speak of her, just as you wanted to hear me; we wanted the same thing, though it would take time to acknowledge this to one another, hence our unease. But there was more to it than this, there was the uncanny resemblance you bore her, which gave me the faintly eerie sensation, in that first conversation, that if I allowed my imagination to drift at will it would be *her* who was with me in that shadowy room—and indeed, when you'd gone, and it grew dark (I stayed in the surgery for hours), I could have sworn she'd been there, the same aura, somehow, lingered that I knew from Jubilee Road. So it was this idea that through you I could glimpse again something of her that made me so desperately afraid that if I said the wrong thing you would vanish, leaving me doubly bereft. "I loved your mother," I said. "She was the most fascinating woman I ever knew." (I didn't say I love her still.) You nodded. You appeared satisfied with this. It seemed to be enough, for the time being.

We talked then of less consequential matters and I was glad of that, it allowed us to be at ease with one another. We talked about the war, and I remember at one point you said, "Oh well, but we always seem to win things, don't we?" I remember thinking such blithe optimism was probably necessary, for a Spitfire pilot. I'm afraid I don't share it.

You rose to leave after half an hour or so and I showed you out. You stood on the front door step and then, seemingly quite on impulse, you turned and said, "May I come and see you again?"

"Of course," I said—a surge of joy and relief—"you're always welcome." A quick nod of gratitude, then you were walking down the drive, small sprightly figure in a smart blue uniform, and I watched you till you'd turned out onto the road and were lost to sight. I stood a moment longer. Dusk was coming on, and the starlings gathered in the trees by the wall at the end of the drive had started their evening chorus. I stepped off the porch and went a small way down the drive, then turned and regarded Elgin against the evening light.

* * *

I'd bought the house in the autumn of 1938, some months after the affair had ended, and the Munich crisis was at its height. I was in a very bad way then, as low as I've ever been, stagnant, depressed, in severe physical pain, and it felt to me as though the world were a distorting mirror in which I discovered only my own reflection: the inexorable drift into war— an echo, merely, of my own imminent disintegration. Elgin changed all that. It enabled me to act. I stood at the end of the drive I remember, the first time I saw it, and gazed in dawning wonder at its steeply gabled roofs, its tall chimneys, its many windows, each one high and narrow, with lancet arches and slender leaded frames. The stone was streaked with salt, and what paint there was was everywhere flaking off to reveal weathered, cracking woodwork beneath. Out in front the grass was knee-high, the hedge untrimmed, and the flower beds overrun with weeds, such that an air of neglect, of decrepitude, almost, clung to the place, but none of that could for one moment detract from the effect it had on me: there was something monumental about the house, something massy, but at the same time it *soared*—the arches, the gables, the steep slate roof and slender chimneys—they drew the eye upward and in doing so aroused a *blaze* of ideas and feelings in me. Oh, it was a romantic house, a profoundly romantic house, it didn't suggest repose, this house, no, it suggested the restlessness of a wild and changeful heart; and its power was immeasurably enhanced by its siting. For Elgin stood close to the edge of a cliff that dropped a sheer hundred feet to black rocks and a churning sea.

Black rocks and a churning sea . . . How many hours have I spent in Elgin dreaming of your mother? Her spirit often seemed more in possession of the house than I was, as though I had haunted it with her memory. I did haunt it with her memory—a museum of nostalgia, this is what I made of Elgin, though at the time I believed it would enable me to forget.

As if the heart ever forgets. But that was what was in my mind that day, as I made my slow way up the drive to the front porch, the roof of which was as steep and pointed as the rest of Elgin's roofs, and knocked on the door. Silence. I knocked again (I've never told you this) and with an audible gasp and a scream of dry hinges and swollen carpentry the door swung open, to reveal an old man in carpet slippers and dressing gown blinking from the shadows at the light of the day. His head was deathly pale and almost hairless, and he peered at me through bleary eyes as with trembling fingers he lifted a cigarette to his bloodless lips. It was Peter Martin. "Yes?" he whispered. I introduced myself and reminded him that we had an appointment. He seemed a little astonished at this, nonetheless he led me into the surgery. "What appears to be the trouble, Dr. Haggard?" he said.

The surgery was the first room off the dark-paneled hallway at the front of the house; a passage led into the back parts, and a carved staircase ascended to the upper floors. I was reminded of the doctor's surgery my father took me to when I was sick as a boy—the examination couch, the glass-doored cabinets full of dressings and medicines, the screens behind which patients undressed—dear boy you've undressed behind those screens yourself! And like the doctor's surgery of my boyhood there were two doors, one giving onto the hallway and the private parts of the house, the other into the waiting room.

Poor old chap. I realized at once that he'd forgotten our appointment and assumed I was a patient—a fair assumption, given the limp, the stick, and my general condition. I corrected his misconception and he showed me over the place: it was as though I'd entered the house I was born in. The furniture was draped in heavy velvet, the mantels were crowded with ornaments and clocks, and heavy lace curtains hung on all the windows. As we moved from room to room he told me about Mrs. Gregor and said he expected that I'd want to keep her on. On the top floors several of the bedrooms were closed up, the furniture sheeted and cobwebs in all the corners, and that's when I started to envision how it all would be once I was installed. "I've let the garden go, rather," he said as we paused at the window on the second floor landing, which looked out over the back of the house onto a jungle of weeds and bushes, more overgrown flower beds, and the sea beyond; "but I daresay you'll be able to take it in hand."

"Yes indeed," I said. Oh, I didn't care about the flower beds or any of that—I just wanted the house! I asked him a few questions about the practice, about what sort of income it could be expected to yield, admitting rights to the hospital, the patients. Old people mostly, he said.

"Fair bit of cancer then?"

"Fair bit."

Then I asked him what he wanted for it, Elgin included. "Hugh Fig didn't tell you?" he murmured.

"No."

We sat outside the back door in old white wicker chairs and talked medicine, a couple of doctors having a drink. He told me a few stories about the practice, odd little tales that usually ended with the words: "Lost him, I'm afraid, nothing I could do." I contained my excitement with difficulty. I learned that this was a community of the frail and elderly who had come to the sea to die, and as the old man rambled on about a nasty case of rheumatic fever he'd treated last winter it occurred to me that for forty years the sick of the district had looked to him for the comfort and support that a physician must dispense when all his technical resources are spent. This is not the science of medicine, this is its art, and I said this to Peter Martin. He wheeled about in his chair and peered at me closely through those bleary old eyes. "Got a family, Dr. Haggard?" he said.

"No." My father died while I was at medical school; my mother when I was a child.

"Not married?"

"No."

"Ah." He sank back. "Anyway," he said, finishing up his tale of the encrusted heart valves, "lost her. Never did have much joy with rheumatic fever."

When it came time to leave we still had not discussed money, or indeed whether he was willing to sell to me, though I believed he was. "Oh, talk to Hugh Fig," he said, as my taxi appeared at the end of the drive, "I'm sure he'll be able to sort it all out."

I thanked him warmly.

"Not at all, doctor," he said. "Too old for it myself anymore. Wife died ten years ago, never quite saw the point of things after that." He turned back inside and closed the door behind him.

Hugh Fig was indeed able to sort it all out, and we quickly came to terms. My mood remained buoyant. I met Mrs. Gregor, and again looked over the house, this time in the full knowledge that it was mine. I was able now to think soberly about where I would sleep, where I would read, and I imagined my late evenings in Elgin, those quiet hours spent listening to music with a book in my lap—how pleasant all that would be, in this large, quiet house! I imagined too how my pictures would hang on the walls, where my books would go, on and on—it is a happy pursuit, the inscription of oneself, as it were, upon some fresh blank tablet like this. Elgin, I decided, would become an expression of myself, or of the self, rather, that I would rebuild here; for I had been shattered, I had been broken in body and in spirit, and I needed a haven to heal in.

Eventually we settled on a date by which the house would be vacated, and I organized the removal of my possessions to Griffin Head. There came a day in the early autumn when I stood in my room in Jubilee Road and surveyed it for the last time, the room that had known such joy, and lately such pain. Books all gone, walls bare of pictures. A single suitcase stood

by the door, and leaning against it my cripple's stick. A faint
last stab of loss, hastily suppressed, and I left. I was becoming
adept at suppressing loss. At the bottom of the stairs I said
goodbye to Desmond Kelly and gave him a fiver. He thanked
me warmly. "You'll come back and see us, will you, doctor?"
he said.

"Oh, I doubt it," I said, "I doubt I'll be back."

I came into Elgin late in the afternoon. There was still much
to do: my boxes were unopened, my books unshelved, my
pictures unhung. All that could wait. I limped through the
empty house, then out to the back. The sea was running
briskly and the sun had begun its descent to the horizon. I
picked my way down the garden path, beating back the weeds
with my stick. I went through the gate in the hedge at the
bottom, and so along the short path to the cliff's edge, where
a set of rickety wooden steps made a steep and perilous descent to the narrow pebbled beach below. The tide was coming in; it foamed and roiled about the black rocks at the foot
of the cliff, then rushed back with a hissing sound, dragging
with it scraps of seaweed and driftwood and other briny det-
ritus. The breeze was stiff, it felt fresh and salty in my face
and in my hair, and carried the cries of gulls from the pier,
which was obscured from view by a jutting headland a hundred
yards or so along the cliffs. There I stood, breathing the good
sea air, and reveling still in a powerful sense of well-being.

After some minutes I decided to attempt the climb down
the wooden staircase to the beach below. I grasped the handrail and took the first step down, but as I did so a sharp twinge
from Spike made me gasp with pain, and I abandoned the
idea, and instead made my way, in no small discomfort, back
up toward the house, and so into the surgery. There I slipped
off my jacket, unfastened my cuff link and prepared to relieve
the pain; a moment later came the familiar glow of spreading
peace, and Spike just faded away.

It was a strange, rather unearthly adventure, that first night

in Elgin. The sky was clear and the moon hung low over the
sea, spilling yellow light on the barely heaving surface. I stood
in the upstairs back bedroom, by the window, with the lights
off, and gazed out toward the horizon for many minutes. The
morphia had silenced Spike, replaced his ache with that pervasive vital warmth that seemed somehow always to compose
me, and enabled me to concentrate my faculties, which
quickly became attuned to the myriad tiny sounds all around
me on the very edge of imperceptibility, all the creaks and
rustles, the sighs and hissing of the woodwork and plumbing
of an old house. It occurred to me then that Elgin was starting
to breathe—it was an odd sensation, uncanny, though curiously exhilarating, the sensation of something old, something
massive that has lain inert and dormant for years, being roused,
shuffling to life again. I limped from room to room in a state
of some excitement, believing, you see, that it was I, Edward
Haggard, who had provided the spark now animating the
frame through which I moved!

It was close to dawn before I felt I could sleep. I had gone
back down through the garden to the cliff, though this time
I didn't try to descend. I watched the sea crashing about the
rocks below, which were shining wetly in the moonlight and
festooned with clumps of bulbed and blackly glistening seaweed. Then I turned, and regarded Elgin for the first time
from the back by night—again that sense of soaring mass,
that upward sweep of the structure, up into the sharp pointed
gables and the high narrow chimneys, a sheen of moonlight
sliding across the slates—I had left every light lit, and the
house shone like a beacon against the night sky. A beacon:
for too long I had been a craft adrift upon a dark and empty
sea, and her the only star I'd had to steer by.

Oh where to begin? Dear James, these few short weeks we've
had—memory has this quality, that it can yield its material
with such remarkable *speed*— a tragedy remembered in the

blink of an eye, a lifetime over a bottle of gin. In these last
few seconds—all this: my relationship with your mother; its
end; the aftermath; you—then strangest of all perhaps, what
happened after we met, my efforts to help you—all of it
vividly present to me *at this moment.* Morphia helps, morphia
excites memory, displays to the inner eye great vistas of experience, lived life, felt life, all in an instant, precise in every
detail. You'd be surprised if I told you how much I looked
forward to our next meeting. Or perhaps you wouldn't—I
know you were eager to talk more about your mother, for what
we had accomplished in that first encounter was merely an
opening of the subject, a breaking of the ice, no more. It was
enough for you to know, that Saturday, that I had loved her.
The rest would come later. As for me, I felt that I must allow
you to dictate how quickly our intimacy developed. You were
the younger man, less sure of yourself in the emotionally
fraught territory that we were about to explore—explorers,
this is what we were, at the start of our journey, and you, I
decided, should set the pace. At the beginning, at least, you
would lead.

You telephoned a few days later. Mrs. Gregor was doing
the spring cleaning I remember, for after talking to you I left
Elgin on my afternoon rounds, and as I climbed into the car
I saw her throw open the window of one of the upstairs rooms
that had been shut up all winter, and the gesture spoke directly
to what I was feeling: my heart was a musty chamber, long
closed, but good clean fresh air was starting to blow through.

You came round to see me after dinner that night. You were
reticent, but it was not the reticence of a weak or uncertain
character, far from it. I felt, rather, that underneath, the character was firmly developed. There was authority, yes, and
hope, too, and a quiet courage—all I've lost, in fact, since
Spike. So while you were often silent, and blushed easily,
there was at the same time a sureness in the way you moved
across a room, the way you sat in a chair, and particularly, in

the way you spoke about what you knew best, which was flight. But at the same time you were so *young!* With your unruly black hair, your clear, burning eyes, your white skin, red lips, the fine clean bone structure of your small dark head—you were still in many ways a boy. I did not take you into the surgery but upstairs to my study and there, after a cursory airman's glance at the sky (evening was shading quickly into night) you sank into an armchair and smoothed the fabric of your uniform trousers while I poured you a glass of beer. "Anything interesting today?" I murmured. I had my back to you, standing by the drinks tray on the table by the door; I glanced over my shoulder and saw you shrug. "Not a lot," you said with a frown, brushing at a speck of dust on your knee.

Later I would learn what it meant, that frown, that clipped dismissive reply: it meant the squadron had lost a pilot. In those first months of the war such loss was still a novelty, but even so, not a thing any of you would make a fuss about. "Poor old Johnny," you might say, "bought it, poor chap"— and that was all. I don't suppose you could afford any greater emotional expenditure than that—a man in a perpetual state of mourning isn't much use in the cockpit of a Spitfire, I can see that.

So I sat down, watched you for a moment, and then put to you the question that had intrigued me since you first appeared in my surgery. "James," I said, busying myself with a cigarette so as to deflect, rather, the weight of the question—"why did you come here?"

"To Elgin you mean?"

I nodded.

You brought together those fine dark eyebrows in a delicate frown—how often I'd seen *her* frown in precisely that manner!—and for a second or two turned your head to gaze at the window at the far end of the surgery. "You loved my mother," you said.

Again I nodded.

"And you knew my father."

"Yes."

"I was never close to him," you said—oh, I could well believe it!—and then you paused; this was not easy for you.

"Go on," I murmured.

"My mother never hid from me the fact that she was unhappy."

All this I knew.

"Sometimes I heard them arguing. I heard your name. I asked her who you were, but she wouldn't tell me."

That scene I could well imagine—I could see her crossing the room, taking your troubled face in her hands, saying, "Now darling, you mustn't ask me questions like that"— she'd spoken the same words to me!

"Then she fell ill, and I felt as though it were connected, somehow. I could never talk to my father about this." Another pause. "I'm sorry doctor, I don't know what it is I'm trying to say. I suppose I feel she left without saying goodbye—is that absurd?"

The way you looked at me then, in an agony of perplexity but at the same time resolute, unafraid—you wanted to understand, even if you risked looking a fool, even if it was painful. You were without guile, this was what charmed and moved me, and I knew it was my responsibility to ease the uncertainty, that sense of incompletion.

"I only joined the squadron a couple of weeks ago," you said, "and it was just by chance I learned that a Dr. Haggard was practicing down here. Stroke of luck, really."

You smiled—James, it was *her* smile!

"Stroke of luck indeed," I said. "But tell me, what do you mean, 'connected'? What was her illness connected with?"

Silence. "I don't know," you said at last. "Connected with the atmosphere at home. With the arguments. With my father being so angry all the time. I felt as if she were being punished."

I was beginning to understand. "Illness isn't a form of retribution," I said gently. "It's not a sign of moral failure."

"Oh I know."

You sighed then, and it tore my heart, that sigh, so great a weight of suffering was in it. "I know that," you said, "so why do I still feel so dreadful about it?"

I had an idea why you felt so dreadful, but I did not voice it. I would have to handle this with great tact and delicacy, I realized. It was time, I decided, to give you what your father never could, some sense of the background of the affair.

I was living at the time, I told you, in a small flat in a large house about a mile from the hospital, in Jubilee Road, one of those long drear north London streets of tall dark houses whose windows, at dusk, uncurtained and unlit, make them look hollow and haunted within. The front door, four or five steps up from the pavement, behind high spiked iron railings, was inset with a panel of stained glass and opened into a dark hallway dominated by a sideboard like a catafalque. At the end of the hallway stairs with threadbare carpeting ascended to the gloom of the upper regions. I had a big, high-ceilinged room on the second floor at the front, overlooking the street, with a fireplace surmounted by a marble mantelpiece and a large mirror. The shelves were crammed with volumes of medicine and poetry, and the faded floral wallpaper was hung here and there with landscapes and sunsets I'd collected as a student. And apart from two armchairs drawn up to the fireplace, and the table I worked at, this was it. There was a small bedroom, almost completely filled by a huge ancient creaking bed; the bathroom was down the hall, and I shared it with the other occupants of the floor, whom I rarely saw as I worked such odd hours.

I was I suppose an unusual creature for a surgical registrar. My father had been the rector of a small parish in Dorset, and I was expected to follow him into the church. I had all the makings of a certain sort of priest—intensely solitary, much

preoccupied with metaphysics, and passionately fond of poetry—and would undoubtedly, had I so chosen, one day have
ministered to a flock of my own. But it was precisely in order
to compensate for what I saw as the rather impractical ten-
dencies in my character, and do some *real* good in the world,
that I'd decided to go into medicine instead. After Oxford I'd
taken the MBBS and then been appointed to the staff of St.
Basil's while I worked for my MD. I was on call thirty-six
hours out of the forty-eight, and was often up all night doing
admissions then assisting in theaters till late in the afternoon.
I won't pretend I was happy. I'd begun to realize I wasn't
meant to be a surgeon, and I'd reason to think that my chief,
Vincent Cushing, to whom I'd been attached since the beginning of August, was coming to the same conclusion.

Oh, he was a tough, bloody-minded character, did you ever
know him? He was like your father. He had no sympathy for
anyone less deft than himself, and he treated surgery like a
branch of mechanics, this is what made him so difficult to
work for. Theaters was up on the third floor at the end of a
white-tiled corridor behind a set of swing doors, with a wash
room where we scrubbed for surgery, which required three
minutes with a hard brush on the backs of the hands, the
palms, between the fingers and halfway up the forearms to
the elbows, and this always left me chapped and sore. I never
had a problem during the simple operations, when I was one
of the two or three doctors performing and could stand over
the incision with a clear view of all that went on, in fact I
quite enjoyed taking out gallbladders, that level of surgery.
It was the complicated procedures I disliked, where five or
six doctors were involved and I'd have the tricky job of holding
the retractors that pulled back the body wall so the surgeon
could get in.

One morning I was desperately tired, having been up all
night in Accident and Casualty, and I was assisting while
Cushing operated. Though I was only an arm's length from

the wound I was excluded from a clear sight of it by a wall of white-gowned backs all stooped over the patient on the table beneath a pair of large, powerful, circular lights. The procedure was a long one, the theater was hot, the atmosphere tense, and after an hour or so everything turned milky—I suppose I must have drifted off. Suddenly there came a loud rap. "More retraction!" barked Cushing, and I was abruptly jerked into the here and now. I gave more retraction. "Too much!" he shouted. "Who is that? Haggard? Wake up, man." The patient was under spinal anesthesia and Cushing was trying to find a bleeder deep in the belly. "Pull the bloody retractor," he cried, "I can't see what I'm doing. No no no no no, you're pulling too hard again, you'll rupture his spleen. Dear God what kind of idiots are they sending me now?" My face, behind my mask, burned with humiliation; impassive eyes gazed at me from other white-masked faces. I let my knees go slack, took a few rapid breaths, and stamped my right foot on my left to stimulate enough vascular tone to stay vertical and awake; fortunately there were no further mishaps.

Afterwards, in the wash room, Cushing eyed me with displeasure as he dried his hands. He was a stocky, impatient man who whistled tunes from the great operas while he operated. "What's the trouble, doctor," he said, "not getting enough sleep?"

"Frankly no, sir," I said. I was buttoning my white coat, about to go back down to the wards.

"Better get used to it. Medicine takes physical stamina, that surprise you?"

"I was aware of that," I said. Damn it, I *had* been up all night!

"You better be aware of it, doctor," snapped Cushing. "You won't last otherwise."

"If I could see what was going on," I retorted, "I could do my job."

"Don't bandy words with me, Dr. Haggard! You're going to have to learn to go days without sleep and perform competently, that clear?"

"Yes sir."

"Good. Because if you can't do that you won't survive. And get your hair cut, doctor!" And with that he flung down his towel and off he went.

The nights were the worst though. Exhausted, I'd write up a history of every patient who appeared, do a physical examination, a white-cell count, a red-cell count, and a hemoglobin, all in the musty closet of a laboratory at the end of the ward that stank of urine and chemicals. Hunched over a stained and battered workbench I'd light a Bunsen burner attached to an ancient gas cock by rotten rubber tubing, then boil the urine gently over the flame until a cloud of protein appeared. Test tubes cracked in the heat, urine spilled, and then, weeping tears of anger and frustration, I'd have to pour more into another tube and start all over again. My back ached from hours spent bending over a bed, a stretcher, an operating table, a lab bench. When I finally got off duty I'd trudge home to Jubilee Road, fall into bed and immediately be asleep, though at times I'd be too exhausted even for sleep, and instead I'd lie there in the darkness and ask myself, why? Why all this pain, all this sickness, what is the *point?* At these times medicine seemed as futile as life itself. For if all one's efforts proved negligible in the face of a steadily increasing volume of human suffering then it was hard to resist the implication of a random godless universe and us, its tenants, mere registers of sensation, specifically pain.

Hardly the most propitious of circumstances for a love affair, then, even if such a thought had crossed my mind, which of course it hadn't—I was always working, and as for your mother, she was a married woman, not only married but married to the senior pathologist and mother of a boy of sixteen! But as luck would have it we encountered one another again quite soon. It happened at the Cushings'; and I suppose you could say that that's when it all properly began.

What had she *done?*—this was what I asked myself as I stood in front of the mirror in the door of my wardrobe in Jubilee Road. Cushing had invited his registrars to dinner, and the senior pathologist and his wife would apparently be among the other guests. I had given little further thought to the woman at the funeral though now, at the prospect of actually meeting her, I experienced a tingle of expectation so visceral my fingers grew moist and gave me trouble with my collar studs. I had no idea what would happen, of course—all this was still inchoate within me, no more than a dimly sensed turbulence in the lower depths. But there was something, I knew there was something, and the picture I had of her lifting her chin as she turned her head in the church that afternoon, and caught my eye and *smiled*—it all came vividly back and aroused in me a powerful emotion I was reluctant to define.

So shortly after seven-thirty, in an elegant suit of evening clothes, with a white silk scarf thrown carelessly around my neck, I left the house on Jubilee Road and set out on foot for the Cushings'. It was a damp, windy night and I had to use my umbrella. This was before Spike of course, and I made good time down those long drear streets of high dark houses, with their hollow, haunted windows; I was still unsettled, and strangely excited. Daphne Cushing I'd already met. She greeted me warmly in the hall. "I knew you'd arrive at just the right moment," she whispered, linking her arm in mine and leading me across to the drawing room, "come in and have a cocktail. I expect you know everybody, we're all St. Basil's tonight." It was a large lofty room filled with dark furniture. Somber curtains hung over the windows. A fire had been lit and long thin flames leaped up from a solid mass of coal. "Ah, Haggard," said Cushing, looking in his dinner jacket like a little polished bullet as he emerged from a murmuring clutch of doctors and wives all in evening dress, "glad you could come. Somebody getting you a drink?" Wagner was playing on the gramophone.

My eye sought her, and found her, instantly. She recognized me of course. She was in an evening gown of oyster satin, cut on the bias and clinging like a glove to her slim form. She moved away from her companion as Daphne Cushing led me to her side. "Fanny, have you met Edward Haggard? He's Vincent's new registrar."

"No," she said, in a voice of smoky velvet, "I don't believe I've had the pleasure."

That night, dear James, your mother took my heart by storm— took it without a struggle. In those first moments I can't have been very articulate, I never am when I'm excited, I tend to become formal, but she understood. With a cocktail in one hand, a cigarette in the other, she lifted her chin and slyly asked me if I was always so disrespectful to the dead. Like you I am a small man, and I'd realized at once that she and I were within an inch or two of each other in height. Daphne Cushing, suspecting nothing, went off to see about the can-apés. "I don't imagine he minded," I said. She smiled that smile I remembered, roguish and conspiratorial, crushing out her cigarette in a large silver ashtray on a stand. As she leaned over, her gown rippled with reflected light from the chan-delier, and what a truly lovely woman she was, I thought— already I was fascinated by her, the pale, perfect skin, the slight, slender figure in the shining sheath of satin. Her dark hair was cut close to the head and gleamed in soft waves in the candlelight. She drew close to me and told me we were seated next to each other at table. Sharp increase of blood pressure in me, and then, laying a hand on my sleeve, she said: "And I don't want to talk medicine, or St. Basil's, or anything remotely connected."

I became aware for the first time of her perfume.

"We can talk about art, or football, or the weather, or whatever you like," she said, "just not medicine or hospitals."

Suddenly I was at ease with her. She found it all as stuffy and tedious as I did. A quiet joy swept through me. "I'm afraid," I protested gaily, "I've thought about little else these last weeks."

"Then you must start now. You're not a complete philistine."

A few minutes later we went through to the dining room. She walked ahead of me, composed and assured, the silk straps of her gown snug against her small perfect shoulder blades. We were indeed seated next to one another, and the talk at the table, as she'd predicted, did revolve around matters medical. But your mother would not allow me to listen, I was there, she said, to entertain her! She asked me about myself and learned I was preparing to take my MD. "And after that?" she said. We were eating soup.

"I suppose," I said, setting down my spoon and dabbing my lips with a napkin, "I shall go into general surgery. Or give myself over to a life of pleasure."

"Pleasure?" she said. She carefully buttered a fragment of bread roll. She gazed absently down the table. "That's rather Twenties of you."

"Oh?"

"I mean, I'd have thought pleasure was a worn-out idea, given the times, wouldn't you?" She turned toward me with lifted eyebrows and sipped her wine.

One often had to think quickly with your mother. She was easily bored, she liked sudden shifts of mood, it was a way she had of testing people. I knew what she was getting at of course, for all the talk at the time was of war. I was not optimistic. With our overextended empire, our faltering industrial output—what chance had we of winning a war with Germany? Thriving, martial, boldly led Germany? I said as much, then added: "But tell me an idea that isn't worn out."

She looked away, apparently contemplating the question. The frown persisted, a delicate vertical wrinkling of the white skin of her forehead.

"Passion," she said.

"Passion?" I was something of a stranger to that idea! "I should have thought that passion, at least, was about pleasure—?"

"Oh no," she said quickly, "it's not about pleasure at all. Passion is very serious. I know you take it lightly, but you'll learn someday what a responsibility it is. It's the best we're capable of, civilized human beings."

Civilized human beings. How strange I would find it, later, to recall a time before I heard her say those words, express that ideal—there seems a curious weightlessness to it now, as though all existence prior to your mother was just a form of floating, a fantastic, ethereal, childlike condition that did end, yes, with the gravity of the responsibility of passion—but all of that was yet to come. "The best?" I said.

"What better?"

"But passion always dies," I said.

"Spoken like a medical man," she said, as our plates were removed. "For you, passion is a disease. It causes suffering, comes to a crisis, and dies."

She turned to me then with that wicked smile of hers and leaned forward, placing her hand on my arm. "Tell me," she said, in a low voice, again sounding like smoke and velvet, "do surgeons make good lovers? Too incisive, I should have thought."

"Try me,' I whispered, and immediately regretted it—I had drunk too much wine! I was much too excited! But she wasn't offended, far from it. She gazed at me a moment, then loosed a peal of laughter that rang round the room like bells. It stopped all conversation, and a dozen faces turned toward us. "I see you're amusing my wife, Dr. Haggard," said the senior pathologist, and conversation resumed.

• • •

All this I told you in my study that evening—not in so many words, but I think I gave you the essence of it. When I'd stopped talking you sat silently with your elbows on your knees, head down, staring at the floor. At least you looked up—and I was enormously touched to see your eyes glistening wetly in the muted lighting of that book-filled room. "She was beautiful, wasn't she?" you murmured.

"Yes," I whispered.

A trembling, tender silence. Then you sat up briskly, pushed a hand through the lick of black hair that had fallen across your forehead, and gazed at me with a frank, clear smile. "Thanks doctor," you said, "I feel better."

You left soon afterwards, but not before promising to return soon. I went back upstairs to my study and spent several hours quietly indulging the memories aroused by the evening's conversation.

Oh James. Love—adult romantic love—I have come to believe is an attitude of passionate devotion to an ideal. Your mother came to represent for me an ideal. She came to seem the very embodiment of grace. Grace: it was manifest in everything about her, it was the ineffable breath of being in all she said, and did, and thought, and felt—her spirit, in a word, she possessed *grace of spirit* and was as incapable of vulgarity as I believe any human being can be. I am a man and a doctor. The body sickens, it goes wrong, it stinks, it rots, it dies. This is where my work is, with the diseases of the flesh. It has become as essential to me as life itself that I animate the pitiful spectacle of sickness and pain with a meaning that transcends mere mortality. The love I conceived for your mother gave me the sole glimpse I have had of the possibility of such meaning, my one thin thread of hope: where before there was only the dark face of nature, with its absolute imperative of disease, suffering and death, now there was grace.

The irony of my life, if not its tragedy, is that I did not understand this until it was too late; only then, as I retraced in memory the vertiginous arc of our affair, and the desperate, terrible brutality of its ending, did I properly come to know what it signified.

The tragedy of my life, then, the failure to understand the nature of love, until it was too late. I don't think I really began to grasp it until that first autumn I spent in Elgin, when the wild winds started to blow. We were up on top of the cliffs of course, exposed to the elements, and I remember how I'd be elated, nightly, by the howling and wailing, sudden huge inexplicable crashes, and great gusts rattling windows and whistling down chimneys, flattening the fire. Around eleven I'd go down to the surgery and see to Spike, then back upstairs, to the back bedroom, which I'd decided to use as my study. I'd select something to put on the gramophone and stand by the window watching the sea, waiting for the morphia to bring relief. Then it would come, and my intellect, like some great bird tethered and pinioned to the earth too long, lifted, and climbed, and soon was soaring, and in the play and shift of vast vague ideas I'd stand there gazing out over the turbulent moonlit sea, and feel the familiar steady glow of peace aroused, the benevolence and serenity that in the normal course of events I rarely experienced, being afflicted so much of the time with pain. I became composed, where before I'd been agitated, I was able to concentrate all that had been scattered and in fragments, see the larger patterns, the higher truths—

Though it was not always so pacific, oh by no means—there were nights my mind played tricks on me, nights about which I have never spoken to you. I remember once, it must have been midnight or later, and the wind was howling, turning from the window back into the room, that dimly lit room of books and thought, and my eye being caught by some small movement in the *wall*, so it seemed. Those old upstairs rooms hadn't been redecorated for eighty years, so the plasterwork was everywhere overspread with a vermiculate network of fine cracks that pleased me in some curious way and that I'd always taken as the random effect of natural aging. Until, that is, the night I caught that movement out of the corner of my eye, and bending to inspect the wall discovered to my utter astonishment that the lines of the cracking formed distinct patterns, distinct *figures*—rich and various clusters of organic motifs, I mean, leaves and tendrils of the vine, in extended scrolls and spirals, and here and there bizarre figures, festoons of fruit, skulls, masks, snakes, and the longer I gazed into the wall, following the intertwining, convoluted lines of the pattern, and identifying newer and stranger grotesques half-hidden in its frenzied sweeps and swirls, the greater became my feeling of unease and excitement—the cracks in the plaster were no mere accidents of time, but *the product of conscious design*. This riot of elaborate organicism, these arches and lobes—they echoed, I realized, the detailing of Elgin's facade, they too expressed the wildness, the changefulness, the enduring vitality of the house—

Though in the morning, when I returned to the study, all I could see was random cracking.

Another time I was in the study late at night when I felt, from somewhere deep in Elgin's bowels, so it seemed, a massive, muffled *thump!* I was at my desk, writing. My head came up. Though it was muffled, there'd been enormous power in that thump—what was it? But before I could make any sense of it there came another one—and another—and another and another and another—and I sat there frozen at my desk, pen poised, in a state of total alarm. With every *thump!* the whole house seemed to shudder, the lights flickered, and for half a minute, maybe longer, it persisted, in a steady, measured rhythm, and I was struck by this single thought, that I was listening to the beating of a heart. But a monster heart—a huge monster heart, pumping and thumping through the shuddering, flickering structure in which I sat. Then it

stopped. As suddenly as it had started, it stopped. A silence—
and a sound, which I can only describe as a *sigh*—as though
the house, or some principle of animation (and respiration)
within it, was releasing breath. It was a long drawn-out sigh,
and it seemed to have an almost sibilant accent to it, a sort
of hiss, as it expired. But what a shock it gave me! I experienced terror, I admit it, there in that shadowy upstairs room,
there was a rapid increase in heart rate, a dilation of blood
vessels, I started to sweat and became aware of the contraction
of my sphincter. I thought the house was falling down! I
thought the entire cliff on which Elgin stood was crumbling,
that the sea, which had been eating into it for so many years—
so many centuries!—had, in hollowing it out, created such a
tortuous, complicated burrow of caves and sea chambers and
passages down there that finally the very foundations had
grown too weak to support the mass above, and the whole lot,
Elgin included, was falling into the sea! But eventually all
was still, and I wiped my clammy face and hands with a
handkerchief and asked myself, what was it? A moment's
thought, and I realized: the generator. Peter Martin had said
something about the generator, but at the time I'd paid no
attention, infatuated as I was with Elgin itself.

The morning after this ordeal I was weary and irritable,
there were deep shadows under my eyes, and in the skin
between and above my eyebrows were etched a series of deep
vertical slanting clefts, like the marks left by lightning on the
bark of a blasted oak. Mrs. Gregor was sensitive. She put my
breakfast before me without even rattling the teacup, but all
I wanted was a cigarette and the newspaper. I told her about
the thumping, and yes, she said, it would be the generator.
She'd get the man in to have a look at it. It was an old house,
this was the problem. Curiously though it endeared me to
Elgin all the more. Houses, I have come to believe, like love,
like nature itself, should not reassure, should not attempt to
soothe, or give comfort, but should, rather, *excite*.

But what was most vivid, those strange howling nights in

the autumn of 1938, to one peculiarly sensitive state of mind—
and it was a rare one, for numerous factors conspired to effect
it—was the first dawning sensation I had of a *presence* within
myself; becoming aware, for some fleeting passage of time,
mere minutes, perhaps, or hours, I never knew how long, of
a sort of *light* that burned in every cell of my body, a light
that did not merely illuminate my being but in a way consti-
tuted it, gave it organization, gave it harmony, meaning and
form—my *soul*, in a word, my spirit. The spirit came through,
and for the first time I knew myself in a physiological sense
to be more than the sum of my parts: an organism, yes, but
not merely that, there was spirit alive in the cells, there was
divinity in my nature, I was pure being created in the very
image of God—

Such were my nights, that first wild autumn in Elgin; my
mornings were more prosaic. Elgin enabled me to act—for
after a period of prostration and inactivity I had resolved to
work once more, to revive the sense of duty, of service, that
had gradually been dying those interminable nights I labored
in the wards of St. Basil's. I knew hospital medicine, and I
knew some surgery, but before I found Elgin I had never
practiced general medicine. Peter Martin came to advise me.
He told me that the backbone of the work was a group of
private patients, elderly retired mostly, who paid a guinea a
visit, though there was a sizable panel list too, for each of
whom I'd get nine shillings a year from the county. He said
that the main thing was to give people something to take
home with them. He used a Brighton pharmacologist for his
preparations, but he didn't have much faith in medicines as
such. "Palliative at best," he said, puffing away at his cigarette, then shuffled across the surgery to the glass-fronted
cabinet and took out a flask of yellow liquid. "Mist Explo,"
he said, "very popular." It was a concentrate made up from
crystals derived from picric acid which I could dilute, two

ounces to eight of water, and dispense to patients with a wide variety of ailments. "Half a crown the surgery visit," he said, "two shillings the medicine, tuppence the bottle."

"Mist Explo?" I murmured, thinking: mumbo jumbo, the man's a witch doctor.

"Vast majority of people who'll come to you," he said, "*vast* majority, doctor, have ailments that fall well within the scope of the body's healing powers. Immense capacity to heal itself, the body, but it's got to be persuaded."

Still I was skeptical. "You'll see," he said, turning away, nodding, ash dripping down the front of his cardigan. He dispensed digitalis for heart conditions but had little faith in that either. "May prolong life a little," he said, and told me a story about an old lady with congestive heart failure and swelling of the legs so gross she could barely move. "Took her digitalis three times a day with a quarter bottle of champagne."

"And?"

"Died. Nothing I could do."

He showed me the three bottles of aspirin he kept in the surgery, in one of which the pills were green, in another pink, in the third yellow. "Make a great business of selecting the most efficacious," he told me, "but they're all the same. We're priests," he said, "that's our function. Give them faith in their own healing powers. Let nature do the work."

Nature. As if nature were exempt from botches.

The morning of my first surgery the waiting room was almost full. Everyone was eager to have a look at the new man, have me inspect their malady. I realized only later that it wasn't Mrs. Gregor's job to send patients in to me, Peter Martin's habit was just to stick his head into the waiting room and say, "Who's next then?" But when she brought me a cup of tea in the surgery shortly before nine, without thinking I asked her to send the first one in. She did as I asked; she didn't want to make things hard for me.

The first was a stout young man in a loud checked suit, sweating profusely. He came in with an air of utter self-confidence, sat down heavily, leaned across the desk and shook my hand. "Morning doctor," he said, "my name is Watkins. I should like you to take me and my family on as patients. I ought to say straightaway, sir, that like a lot of other people I've been through hard times, in fact if it hadn't been for Mrs. Watkins I tell you straight I should've gone under, wonderful woman she's been. I may have run up a bill or two that should've been paid sooner but that's all over now. I'm in the scrap metal trade, and business is looking up at last. War coming, see? I shall very soon be able to hold my head up anywhere, and let me say right now that you shall be paid in full and prompt for your attendance. As soon as the bill comes in it'll be paid, I promise you that. I thought we'd better understand each other man to man right at the start, so I won't waste no more of your time. It's my balls. That's my trouble and my only trouble. Swell up with water every so often."

I reminded myself that I was here to serve. I looked up the man's file and found that Peter Martin had regularly tapped his hydrocele, a collection of fluid round the testicle. I told Mr. Watkins the next time he had trouble of that sort he should come in and I'd see to it. Apparently satisifed that our relationship was off on the right foot he vigorously shook my hand and marched out.

I saw several more patients before lunch. One disturbed me particularly, an ill-nourished young woman with pale lips and chlorotic skin who told me a sad tale of too many children in too small a house, and an unemployed husband depressed and drinking. Her own will to survive was clearly flagging. She was grossly anemic, so I prescribed iron, though this would barely begin to address her problems, and we both knew it. Another woman came in with a nasty case of pin knee—inflammation of the patella—from scrubbing floors. So I made up a kaolin poultice, poured boiling water on it and bound up the knee, then had her sit in the waiting room while the heat drew up the sepsis. She became upset. She was a char, she told me, and if she couldn't get down on her knees to scrub floors she couldn't work, and if she couldn't work she wouldn't eat. I told her just to sit still and when the time came I'd lance the abscess and all would be well. She went back into the waiting room and I called in the next patient. By the end of the morning I was thoroughly exhausted and Spike was throbbing painfully.

Mrs. Gregor wasn't ready with my lunch so I wandered out into the garden and down to the gate, where I lit a cigarette and turned back to look at the house. It cheered me. The sight of it lifted my spirits, reminded me why I'd chosen to come here. It was a windy day, the sky was clear, there was a strong bite of salt in the air, and Elgin was looking very gray, very lean and spiky, it seemed to be all juts and angles, all points and edges, less mass than plane. I smoked my cigarette and felt somewhat strengthened in my resolve; the first man, Watkins, had laid a chilly finger on my heart with his bland and cheerful "War coming, see?" I did see, oh I did. When I went back in Mrs. Gregor told me there was still someone in the waiting room. The woman with the pin knee! I'd forgotten all about her! I took off the poultice, and the knee has pussed up nicely, so with a sterilized needle I lanced it there and then, and sent her on her way.

After lunch I made house calls. I'd bought a motorcar from a man in Griffin Head, a dark green Humber that I was assured would be reliable. Nancy Hale-Newton was the widow of a colonel and lived in a large house called the Elms with her daughter Marjorie, a schoolteacher. Marjorie took me upstairs to her mother's sickroom. The curtains were drawn against the light and Mrs. Hale-Newton lay in bed, her complexion drained of all healthy color and turned a leaden grayish-yellow, the flesh so wasted the skin hung loose on her bones. A claw-like hand fluttered up from the counterpane and a cultivated but weary voice spoke: "Where's Peter Martin?"

I put down my black bag and Marjorie said, "Dr. Martin

retired, Mummy, don't you remember? This is Dr. Haggard."

"Haggard? Never heard of him. What happened to your hair, Haggard?"

"Good afternoon, Mrs. Hale-Newton," I said. "I'm Edward Haggard. I've taken over the practice from Peter Martin."

"I like Peter, he's a good man, he tells me the truth. You speak the truth, Haggard?"

"I try to."

"Evasive answer. You don't need to pretend with me, I've made my peace. Couldn't accept it at first, created a terrible fuss. Poor Peter, what a time I gave him! Face the darkness, Nan, he'd say, and I'd say, what darkness you old fool—I feel fine!"

The voice trailed off. Silence and shadows. I prepared a needle and asked the dying woman whether she wanted it now. "Yes," she murmured, "yes I do. I won't be going out just yet, Marjorie, I haven't finished with the injections."

On our way downstairs Marjorie Hale-Newton asked me what I thought her mother meant. I knew only too well. "She means," I said, "that she's at least getting pleasure from the morphia."

"Oh I know she is," said Marjorie. "She gets very impatient with me if I make her wait."

"Don't make her wait," I said. "Let her have it when she wants it."

Driving home that day I reflected that the practice of general medicine, and a firm discipline of work, and contact with ordinary people, with ordinary problems—this is how you treat a broken heart. Before I found Elgin I'd been constantly susceptible to terrible sudden powerful gusts of emotion that always left me devastated. For I missed your mother so intensely I could almost feel her presence—sometimes, if Spike was bad, I did feel her presence—and to suppress these attacks much psychic effort had to be expended. Occasionally

I succeeded, more often I failed. I found that if I tried to abort a stream of memories before it had progressed very far I could often spare myself a harrowing; though it soon became apparent that if I *did* suppress them, the feelings weren't dissipated but instead were merely dammed, as though in a reservoir, and when the floodgates opened—as invariably they did, sooner or later—then out it all poured, with torrential violence, leaving me weak, racked, sobbing, and unutterably wretched. To lose myself in hard work, far from London, among people who knew nothing of me or of her, and where there were no associations to trigger pain: this was how I thought I could get over it. I've never told you just how grim it really was, and with what success—or lack of it—I managed to deal with the loss of your mother. Why not? Why didn't I tell you how it really was, for me? Because, I suppose, you began to manifest your own pathology, and when that happened it preoccupied me almost to the exclusion of all else.

But this was the pattern of my days, morning surgery, house calls in the afternoon, evening surgery, on call for emergencies. I'd take one afternoon off a week and the occasional weekend. I soon realized that much of what Peter Martin had told me was essentially correct, that general practice involved a little surgery, a little medicine, and much reassurance and advice. I too became an advocate of Mist Explo.

And what, meanwhile, of my heart? Was it healing, as I'd thought it would, as a function of this fine big house, the care of a good woman, the practice of general medicine? As time passed I began to think it was. I began to think I was leaving the affair behind me, getting it out of my system. There were the odd twitches and twinges, but nothing I couldn't cope with. I was feeling better. I was forgetting her. Oh, I was fooling myself! I'd been briefly in remission, that's all, and this sad fact was brought home to me most vividly one afternoon that winter, on my way to see a patient.

I was driving along the seafront when I saw her. She was

turning up a side street, so the glimpse I had of her was partial
and lasted no more than a second, but it was *her*, it was your
mother—the way she walked, the way she dressed—she was
in a black fur coat—the whole air of the woman—it was her,
it had to be her, and I pulled over to the curb, climbed out
of the car, grabbed my stick and hobbled after her in great
haste, despite the howls of protest from Spike. Your mother!
Here in Griffin Head! What was she doing here? She was here
for me, obviously, she was *coming back to me!*

And of course it wasn't her. When I finally caught up with
her she was, yes, an attractive, fashionably dressed woman of
your mother's age, and she handled my apologies in the most
charming manner, she was piqued and amused at my error,
and even made a moue of mock chagrin that she wasn't whom
I'd thought her—but she wasn't your mother, and I retreated,
I limped off, cursing myself for a fool, for it wasn't, I confess,
the first time it had happened though it was the first time I'd
been so utterly convinced that it was her. It shook me badly,
the whole experience, and late that night I was still thinking
about it, thinking about the moment when with beating heart
I'd touched her shoulder and she'd turned, though by that
time, in my imagination, she'd become your mother, it was
your mother who'd turned, her face open and shining, and
pressed herself against me, and gripped the collar of my overcoat, and touched my face, and whispered hello, and why
should the memory of her clutching my collar and pulling me
to her like that have affected me so, was it the slimness of
her fingers and the way they tugged at me like a child's? Oh,
I did myself no good that night, no good at all, limping round
Elgin and weeping like a boy as I tortured myself with the
idea of the woman in Griffin Head that afternoon being her,
of her coming back to the car with me and returning with me
to Elgin—I showed her round the house that night, I took
her (slim phantom) into every room, then later we walked to
the cliff and stood gazing at the sea, and I remember every

word we said to each other, for I've lived every moment of it
a hundred times over, and wrung from every moment every
last ounce of sweet feeling it offered before passing on and
allowing the hours to unfold to their own exquisite pattern.
Near dawn I drank a couple of glasses of gin, which calmed
me, and then I was able at least to contemplate sleep.

Your mother. Or rather, *not* your mother—frequently, in the
days that followed my encounter with the wrong woman, I
limped back and forth across the upstairs back bedroom in a
state of rage—rage at my own folly, my own ineptitude, my
own damn weakness, impotence, fatuity—had I not left London precisely to prevent this sort of thing from occurring? Had
I not bought Elgin precisely because it was untouched by
memories of your mother, because it was free of those associations so rife in London, stabs of loss that came with each
chance glimpse of a bit of the world once shared with her? I
knew now there'd be no easy relief from the pain aroused
from within, the pain I'd foolishly thought almost extinct. At
every passing moment, so it seemed, in the days following,
some faint cool shadow rose unbidden into consciousness, the
image, perhaps, of her going before me into dinner at the
Cushings', or slipping off a shoe, in the quiet of the saloon
bar of the Two Eagles, to rub a silken foot against my calf,
or murmuring to me with languid affection from my bed in
Jubilee Road—time, I'd thought, would lay these inner
ghosts, and surely, to have left the city where the affair had
taken place, surely this must help the process of time, help
begin to heal the rawest of the wounds, ease the more fero-
cious, the more savage and implacable of the hurts I had
sustained? But no, apparently not. Apparently I was not yet
to enjoy the luxury of a simple melancholy, not yet to know
resignation, and the ability to recall the loved one's memory
with tenderness rather than pain. No, apparently I was to
twist and thrash and flail about a little longer.

I remember one day sitting at the table picking at my lunch (since Spike I'd become a very light eater), feeling weary and dispirited and wondering if I'd made a ghastly mistake in taking on the practice, the house, all of it, and I remember glancing up at Mrs. Gregor as she quietly poured me a cup of tea. Her calm face cheered me. She knew I was in pain; though she said nothing, I could tell she knew, and I felt her concern, and her sympathy. She seemed to be telling me that all would be well. And I remember thinking, no, I will not be lonely. I will not allow myself to be overwhelmed by hopeless longing for something that has ceased to be real. But even as I thought this a small voice said, oh, but it is real—your feelings are real, your pain is real, your loss is real—and as if he'd been waiting for just this to happen, Spike delivered an especially vicious jab, which sent me hobbling back to the surgery.

Later I again tried to rally my spirits, and reflected that if I was to avoid sinking into a bog of maudlin emotion I'd have to develop a firmer mental discipline. It occurred to me that I couldn't simply wait for time to heal me, I would have to set about deliberately healing myself, for it was absurd to be the slave of feeling. Feeling, I told myself, is only one facet or dimension of experience, and by what law must it predominate over the rest?

For several days I held to my resolve. I did not permit myself to think about your mother. When I did, when I found myself caught up in some sweet passage, intoxicated with some memory, I abruptly shut it down, and turned my attention elsewhere. It was not easy, nor was it altogether successful, for if I banished her from my waking mind she merely waited till nightfall, and it was very much harder to keep her out of my dreams.

But I tried. And eventually there came a period of several days when I did not suffer. I began to think it was working. I began to think that my refusal to indulge the reveries and memories and night-dreams that thronged about the doors and windows of consciousness, beseeching entry—my refusal to admit them, I thought, was gradually stilling the storm and allowing me to inch toward peace once more. Peace—peace of mind—where I could contemplate your mother and the few brief months we'd had without having to wage this constant terrible warfare with the armies of my own unconscious mind, whose sole objective so it seemed was to lay waste to my heart and leave me howling for the woman I loved like an orphaned child amid the rubble of a bombed city.

Oh James. A lifetime remembered in a bottle of gin; a tragedy in a grain of morphia. How clearly I see it all now, this drama, this story—the design of the thing a journey, of still-uncertain destination; or perhaps a wheel, within whose spokes and arcs pain and suffering appear not as manifestations of futility but as the ground or soil or compost of the spirit whence new growth springs: for we rot and rise, and without pain there can be no light. And the figures, the characters, all etched in sharp relief against a blood-red sky: your mother, Ratcliff, yourself—me—the others, less vivid, whose fates are somehow intertwined with these. One, curiously, was a dying boy I treated in St. Basil's, a young workingman called Eddie Bell, who was in the last stages of tuberculosis. He shouldn't have been on a surgical ward, but we'd found a lump in his lung and taken out a rib. Not that it did much good. The disease was progressing faster than the thorax could heal, and Eddie grew paler and thinner by the day.

I suppose it's not surprising that I should think of him now, for he, like you, would die in my arms. But oh, poor Eddie! There was something about the boy, and the way he faced death, that made a deep impression on me. I'm a doctor, I've seen a good deal of death, but there are always those who shatter your detachment and wring your heart and make you pray for a miracle. Eddie Bell was a clean, decent lad with a wife and a baby, and it seemed the cruelest thing that he should be taken so young. One night I was at his bedside when he coughed suddenly and blood came welling into his mouth. He struggled up, this thin, white ghost of a boy, ethereal, almost, against the sheets, and spat it out to keep from choking. It made a dramatic splash of claret on the bed-clothes, and I called for a nurse. We screened his bed and I wiped away the rubbery clots of blood and mucus from his mouth while the sheets were changed. "Will it be tonight?" Eddie murmured, when I had him comfortable again, and I couldn't lie to him, I nodded, and said: "Yes Eddie, maybe tonight." There was no way to stop the bleeding, so no point in giving a transfusion. Close to dawn I made up a needle of morphia. "Doctor," he said—he was very weak, and I had to cradle him in my arms in order to give him the injection— "before you give me that, promise me there'll be no post-mortem. I told my wife I'd come to her clean and unscarred."

I promised, of course I did.

Then I gave him the morphia and he became soporific. The bleeding continued until his poor wasted lungs could no longer gather enough oxygen to sustain life, and his skin whitened to the color of an embalmed corpse before my eyes. I laid him back down and covered him with the sheet. Just as I emerged from between the screens Cushing appeared at the end of the ward, accompanied by McGuinness, my fellow registrar. Down they came, white coats swirling, with Sister beside them, and we gathered round the bed. "I'll be curious to see what happened to that abscess," said Cushing. "Get him down to Pathology, will you, Haggard? Tell Ratty Vaughan we want to have a look at the lungs."

All I could think of was the promise I'd made to Eddie just a couple of hours before. I mentioned it. Cushing snorted; he told me it was a damn silly thing to do, making promises to a man who wouldn't last the night. "Oh, promise him the world, if you want to," he then said, "but don't for God's sake think you have to keep it."

"But is a postmortem really necessary?"

This was not wise. McGuinness gazed at the ceiling, Sister slipped off down the ward. "You imagine, Dr. Haggard," said Cushing, in tones of the iciest courtesy, his eyes bright with scorn, "I wish to look at the boy's lungs for fun?"

"No sir."

"To divert myself?"

"No sir."

"Thank you. I'm gratified at the high regard you appear to hold for my sense of professional responsibility."

Oh damn you, Cushing, I thought, as I weathered a few more blasts, damn you and your hard cold surgical medicine, what room is there for caring and humanity and compassion in your sort of medicine? I left the ward a little later. I had twelve hours before I was on call again, and I intended to sleep. It was just striking noon as I came out onto the steps of St. Basil's. The day was wet and dismal. I stood there in the drizzling rain, exhausted, depressed, and without an umbrella. I turned up my collar and prepared to run for the bus. "You'll catch your death," someone said. I turned. It was your mother.

She was wrapped in a black fur coat with a huge collar and pouch sleeves, holding a large umbrella, and on her head a closely fitted, dark green, turbanlike hat jabbed with a parrot's feather. She'd been in the hospital, she said, "doing good works." Her eyes were moist as though she'd been crying; she seemed a sad, rather fragile creature in all that black fur, but even as she looked me over, looked me up and down, a smile began to form, and her spirits visibly rose. "You look ghastly," she said. "Shall we go and have a drink?"

The hotel was an elegant Georgian building where they seemed to know her well. She surrendered her umbrella, but not her fur, and led me across a marble-floored hall to a large, comfortable lounge furnished in the baroque manner. We settled ourselves in a pair of wing chairs with curved legs, beneath a high ceiling divided into panels containing foliate and shell motifs. A waiter silently materialized beside her chair. "What will you have, doctor?" she said, opening her coat. I asked for a gin and tonic, and she'd have one too. Then she sighed, and said, "All this rain, I do find it so depressing. I wanted to tell you how much I enjoyed meeting you the other night, was it very dreadful for you?" As she said this she groped in her handbag for cigarettes.

"On the contrary," I said. I could feel the fatigue and depression of the last hours lift. I lit her cigarette for her. "Thank you darling," she said—darling!—then: "What have you been up to?"

"Practicing hospital medicine," I said, "but I wouldn't want to bore you with that."

"Oh," she said, "I don't think you could bore me, a man who'd dedicate his life to pleasure." A small smile as she glanced at me through half-closed eyes, then, before I could reply: "Who was the last patient you saw?"

"Eddie Bell, plumber's mate. Consumption."

"Poor fellow," she said. "How is he?"

"Dead," I said, as the gins arrived.

The waiter was bending over the table between us, setting down the glasses. For several moments we did not speak. The waiter moved away.

"Sorry," I said, "didn't mean to be blunt."

"Oh don't worry about that," she said. "Living with Ratcliff all these years, death is an old friend." She sipped her gin. "I daresay he's told you that the science of medicine is built upon the postmortem?"

"I'm afraid your husband was never a teacher of mine."

"Lucky you. I'm sorry, I don't mean to embarrass you with my disloyalty." She looked away. There was a brief silence. She really had the most exquisite profile, the clear brow, the small fine nose with its delicate, paper-thin nostril, the white white flesh of her throat! I told her more about Eddie Bell,

and the promise I'd made him, and what had happened when
Cushing came.

Her eyes settled fondly upon me. I thought there was languor in them, though in fact (this she told me later, when our
early impressions of one another were an eager topic of conversation) she was conscious not of languor but of admiration.
She thought I'd been brave to stand up to Vincent Cushing,
and she liked me for it. "How marvelous," she sighed, "to
hear a doctor speak about medicine as a moral activity."

"Clinical work," I said. I think I understood the drift of
her thinking, and felt slightly alarmed—I hadn't meant to
impugn Cushing's *morality!* I made some demurral, said something vague about the need for research; ironic, considering
my recent run-in with the man. She wasn't having any of it.
An impatient snort of scorn. "But don't you wonder," she
said, "what it is makes men spend their working lives poking
through the diseased bits of dead bodies? God, there I go
again. Don't answer that. Here I am telling you all my secrets,
it must be the drink, it always goes to my head before lunch."
She asked me what the time was. "So late!" she cried. "I had
no idea! I must fly!"

We parted on the steps of the hotel. The rain had stopped
and a watery sun was trying to break through the clouds.
Suddenly the turmoil of London was upon us, the buses and
taxis and crowds, and suddenly I felt extremely weary; I had
been almost two days without sleep. Your mother was drawing
on her gloves. "I did enjoy that," she said, turning to me.
"Oh, you're exhausted. Take a taxi home, please."

"Maybe I will," I said, though I knew I wouldn't.

"Goodbye Dr. Haggard."

"Goodbye Mrs. Vaughan."

We shook hands.

Reflecting, later that night, on our conversation, I thought of
what your mother had said to me about Ratcliff. And I won-

dered—could I tell you about that revealing disclosure of hers, without alarming you unduly? For how odd it was, I'd thought, that she should have said what she did about your father's work, and with such passion! Or so it had seemed to me at the time (of course I knew nothing then of your parents' marriage)—my story had aroused anger in her not toward Vincent Cushing, but toward her husband, toward Ratcliff. Could I say this to you? Would it help? Or were you (it suddenly occurred to me) on *his* side? Later she told me that she'd been late for her lunch appointment and had then wandered round the National Gallery all afternoon, "somewhat *distraite*," she said, though at the time she couldn't think why. She didn't get back to Plantagenet Gardens until after six, and when she walked in through the front door your father was coming down the stairs dressed for dinner. "Darling, have you any money in your pocket?" she said. "I've a taxi outside."

"Leaving again?" said Ratcliff.

She could be very funny sometimes. She told me how, on her way back into the house, Ratcliff had called her from the drawing room, where he was standing in front of the fire turning the pages of the *Lancet*. She paused in the doorway—I can imagine the expression on her face, her fingers busy with the delicate task of removing her hat—as Ratcliff put to her his big question. "Had you forgotten the Piker-Smiths?" he said, without looking up. And of course she had! She had completely forgotten the Piker-Smiths! She hadn't been in the kitchen all afternoon, so Iris would be hysterical and the meal a fiasco! Ratcliff let the question sink in then gazed at her over the top of his spectacles. But she wouldn't give him the satisfaction, she told me. "Of course not," she said. "Fascinating couple. He told me such an interesting thing about bowel tumors last time, I must remember what it was. Who could forget the Piker-Smiths?"

"Now where were we?"

You'd telephoned to ask if you could come up to Elgin and

talk to me more about your mother. It was almost two weeks since our last conversation, and it had occurred to me that you might not come back. You arrived just after my late surgery, rather breathless, having come all the way up the hill on a bicycle. It was a lovely evening, shortly after the battle of Dunkirk, I remember, for black smoke from blazing oil tanks had been blowing across the Channel all day, though by the time you appeared the wind had changed direction and the evening was glorious. As you pulled off your bicycle clips and then, panting and smiling, pushed a hand through your disheveled hair, I suggested we take our drinks outside. "Lovely," you said.

We sat in the old white wicker chairs out on the paving stones by the back door, a low table between us and on it a bottle of gin, a bottle of tonic, two glasses and an ashtray. The sun was going down, the sky was a mellow symphony in pastel shades of blue and gray with one solitary rag of cloud angling down toward the sea, its underside lit by a vivid pink rash. Beyond the paving stones the garden was a blowsy profusion of unmown grass with a large rosebush overflowing its trellis and heavy with white flowers. "Where were we?" you said. "We were at a dinner party, doctor, and my mother was being witty."

Oh dear, I can be so clumsy. There was such harmony and contentment in that evening hour, as we watched the sky change color, and the sun descended to a sea of polished steel, I forgot my decision to let you make the running—I was, I realize, too fervent in the depiction of my feelings, it is a failing of mine. I told you how, at the end of the evening, as I was getting into my overcoat in the hall, she had approached me and asked me with a small smile, with just a hint of *innuendo* in it, if I was off in pursuit of 'fresh pleasures.' "No," I told her, "I've had quite enough pleasure for one evening."

"You must take me with you next time," she said, "I never seem to get any pleasure anymore." At that moment your father came up with her fur coat. She thanked him, then said:

"I was just telling Dr. Haggard how we never seem to have any pleasure these days."

"Pleasure?" said Ratcliff, glancing at me with a jovial expression that can hardly have been sincere. "My wife has never shown an interest in pleasure, she's much too busy. I hope you're not corrupting her, doctor."

I know a growling animal when I hear one; James, this was a man with a threat! "Oh, I know little about pleasure," I said, having no desire, at the time, to antagonize the senior pathologist. "I'm just an amateur."

"An Englishman and an amateur!" cried Ratcliff, with that familiar bark of laughter. He had a cigar between his teeth and he was mellow with brandy. "Like myself." Here he laid a hand upon my shoulder, a gesture apparently of warm male complicity, but I knew better.

"I'm surrounded by amateurs," murmured your mother, "are there no qualified sybarites in the house?"—at which point Daphne Cushing came gushing in and the whole thing collapsed into babble and chat.

But what I remember, when I described this scene to you, was the troubled expression that appeared on your face. Had I gone too far? Had I hinted inadvertently at what must only be gradually revealed, had I given it all away? And it was only then that I properly realized how difficult it would be to tell you the story of our affair, for no child can listen dispassionately to an account of his mother's infidelity. But because it was essential (I felt) that you understand, I knew I had to do it, but with a sort of opaque clarity, a delicate, oblique candor . . . I paused, and you rose to your feet, took a few steps down the path and stood there silently gazing at the sun as it sank behind a horizon line sharp as a blade. Without turning you said: "So did she throw herself at you?"

"Oh good God no!"

Had I given you that impression? I pulled myself out of my chair and went to you. You were blushing wildly, angry and confused like a hurt child—I felt a wave of warm protective sympathy rise within me, and I caught you by the shoulders. "James, James, no, it wasn't like that, forgive me, I didn't mean to suggest that for a moment, there was nothing like that, nothing like that at all"—and I gazed into your eyes with as much earnest conviction as I could muster, and held your shoulders firmly, and at last saw you soften. "Believe me," I whispered.

You wanted to be convinced; you shrugged off the terrible suspicion that had sprung into your mind. "Sorry."

"Nonsense," I said, dropping my hands and limping back to my chair. "Nothing to be sorry for. Finish your drink. Have another."

"No," you said, "I must be off." You hesitated. "Doctor, I don't know if you'd be interested, but there's a sort of a do on up at the mess."

Now you were reticent, embarrassed at what had just happened between us—you were still blushing! Oh James, I warmed to you more with every moment we spent together— you had her face and her grace but you had yet to acquire her composure. "Are you inviting me to a party?" I said.

"Well, yes, actually."

"Where and when?" I said, and when you told me I said that if I wasn't on call I would certainly come. I was flattered; I was also curious to see how you were with the rest of the squadron. I'd met a couple of the other pilots and they seemed a good deal more hearty than you, they lacked that moody complexity that so intrigued me about you. Was this, I wondered, a source of discomfort to you—were you the butt of humor—did they pull your leg—?

What happened next? She came to my room. I was never able to tell you about her coming to my room—how could I? Though maybe you guessed. It was late 1937, autumn had slipped into winter, the weather was damp and chilly and the frail and elderly with their rheumatism, their influenza, their arthritis came tramping through the doors of St. Basil's, seeking care. One night I was in the flat in Jubilee Road, having been on duty for forty-eight hours straight. The gas fire was lit but it wasn't enough, and I was wearing a jersey, a cravat, and my lined paisley dressing gown. I'd had a perfectly bloody day. Cushing had told me I'd never make a surgeon and again I'd seriously asked myself if he was right. There was a certain untutored deftness with fine instruments that I seemed simply to lack. I paced the room, hands plunged deep in my pockets, smoking, worrying, trying to stay warm. Someone knocked at the door. "Come in, Desmond," I shouted.

The door opened. "It's not Desmond"—those familiar tones—and I whirled round: it was your mother. We were immediately in each other's arms—her very *being there* shattered whatever thin crusts of reserve and propriety still stood between us! We clung to one another. "Something has happened," she whispered.

"I know."

Something has happened. Dear James, never, I think, can three simple words have engendered such joy in a man's heart. We clung to one another in the middle of the room, rocking slightly; eventually we came apart. For a moment or two we hovered there, stranded in some odd void between intimacy and decorum: something had happened, yes, but whatever it was, it was yet to be assimilated. She took my face between her fingers then turned away. She drifted to the window, pulled aside the curtain, and glanced out. I think I must have offered her a drink.

We sat in the armchairs, pulled up close to the gas fire. She kept her coat on and wrapped her fingers round her glass and stared into the thin hissing flames. Usually so voluble, she was now silent and I, with my initial excitement checked, rather, by her strange, distant mood, watched her, and waited, ready to take my cue from her. "I'm sorry it's so cold in here,"

I said at last. She glanced up. "Were you listening to the news?" she said.

"Yes. I'm rather afraid we're in for it."

"War with Germany. What a beastly idea."

"I'm so glad you came. I keep thinking about you."

"Yes, I know." She frowned.

"You know?"

She nodded. "It's happened to me as well."

I wanted to take her in my arms there and then and cover her perfect face, and her throat, and her breasts with kisses. She reached for my hand. She held it in both of hers and gazed at me with great seriousness. "What are we to do?"

I saw no problem. "Celebrate?"

She wasn't amused. She stared into the gas fire. Then she shook her head and rose abruptly to her feet. "I must go," she said.

"No, don't."

"I must. This is foolish. What can come of it? I shouldn't have come here, it was a stupid impulse."

"It was a wonderful impulse. Please sit down. Five minutes."

She hesitated. "Five minutes."

Five minutes.

Traces of her perfume clung to my dressing gown. I noticed it as soon as she'd gone, as I wandered about the room, touching things, my thoughts and emotions in turmoil. I brought the material to my nose, and smelling her perfume awakened the memory of touching her, the warmth of her slim body beneath the fur coat when I first slipped my hands in under it. I became aroused all over again, and felt suddenly trapped, so I threw on my hat and overcoat and ran downstairs and out into the blustering raw night and began to walk.

I never knew quite where I walked or for how long. All I could recall, later, were dark streets of large houses lost in gusting sheets of rain, water streaming in the gutters, the occasional bowed figure hurrying by in the blur of a streetlight, umbrella slick with rain—striding forward through the night, my hat pulled low over my forehead and my overcoat flapping about me, I did not feel the cold and damp, for I was wrapped in the heat of erupting emotions that didn't even *begin* to subside until I turned at last into a small pub called the Two Eagles, not far from Jubilee Road, and stood at the counter of the saloon bar, dripping wet and still in high excitement, and bought a large gin. Only then did I articulate it: I love her.

This produced dazed bewilderment, the very idea of it, and I found a small table near the fire—the room was deserted—sat down and took off my spectacles to wipe them on my handkerchief, and gazed at the burning coals and told myself again: I love her. I contemplated the fact. How odd it was. Funny really. How had it happened? Small miracle, considering, but there you are, there you have it. I love her. At last I looked up, looked around, realized how wet I was; then the clock behind the bar caught my eye. I should have been at St. Basil's twenty minutes ago!

The ward was in darkness when I got there, and silent but for some wheezing and snoring and the odd soft moan. McGuinness was with the night sister in her office. He had little to tell me, and when I'd apologized for keeping him waiting he struggled into his overcoat and prepared to leave. "Wet out, then," he said; I must have looked like a drowned rat. "Filthy night," I said vaguely.

Filthy night—yes, to McGuinness it would look like a filthy night, to all the world it was a filthy night, but to me, to Edward Haggard, no, not a filthy night, a golden night, a blessed night. In the hours that followed I would find moments here and there, little islands of grace amid the darkness of sickness and injury, when this immense miracle of the heart became once more vivid to me. For the first time in my adult life I knew I loved a woman.

It began to rain again shortly after midnight, and it kept up almost until dawn. The ward was quiet, and I took some minutes to stand on the steps between the great portals at the hospital entrance, my white coat whipping about my legs, and my mind spreading out across the city like a vast winged god. Strong winds blew; there was no moon, only heaped banks of low cloud, and the streets of London flashed and shone in the downpour; every few moments the wind flung volleys of rain at the windows of sleeping houses, and embers hissed in deserted fireplaces as the rain found its way down chimneys. It tumbled in torrents along gutters and into drainpipes, it went flooding down drains. What few people were about in the city scurried with their heads down from doorways to cabs, their umbrellas ravaged and broken in an instant. It was the same storm system that had been lashing the south coast for days now; in the capital, citizens turned uneasily in their beds, ancient race memories awoken by the violence of the weather battering at their windows and doors. Your mother has described to me her state of mind that wild night. She did not attempt to sleep. She sat on the padded stool in front of her dressing table, she said, removing her makeup, in her silver robe. A fire burned in the grate, two table lamps gave off a low, warm glow. The room was deeply carpeted, the curtains were thick. There was warmth, safety and comfort in this room, but the fingers of danger plucked at her throat—and she *liked* it, she told me, she liked it, it made her feel alive. A curious mood, she told me, with this excitement, this restlessness upon her, and from time to time she went to the window and pulled aside the curtain and watched the storm sweeping about the houses opposite, and all along the pavement the bare branches of the big old chestnuts flailing in the wind. Then she turned and wrapped her arms about herself, and closed her eyes, arousing in herself the memory of deep and recent sexual pleasure.

For I had been a good lover to her. She had risen from the armchair and wordlessly taken my hand and led me into the bedroom, where without haste, and keeping her eyes upon mine, she had begun to undress, and I of course had done the same. It was with some care that she laid her clothes and underwear on my chair. Then we climbed in together under the sheets. My heart rate was very high indeed. I took her in my arms and her skin was soft as silk against my own. I began kissing her face and her throat, and when I lifted my head from her breasts, she saw (she told me later) my eyes, and never, she said, did she imagine she would forget their expression at that moment, the utter glut of feeling, the *love* that was in them. Something in me cried out when I entered her, and in the few timeless moments that followed I knew a sense of fusion and completeness that I had never experienced before, and never will again until I die. It was the first time I had properly made love to a woman.

Later, in her room, she heard Ratcliff coming up to bed, heard him cross the landing at the top of the stairs, then go straight to his room, and this was unusual, for it was his habit to tap at her door and open it a crack and whisper to her to sleep well. She liked that he did that, she told me, but tonight he did not, and this made her feel grateful and uneasy at the same time. Suddenly the world seemed fragile. Suddenly it all seemed to shiver, as though great explosions were occurring three streets away. She leaned against the wall of her room, she said, pressed her body full against it, to feel how solid it was. She sat down at the dressing table and stared at her own reflection. We must be careful, very very careful; we must never make a mistake; there are ways of doing these things. There is danger here, but we can control it. All this she told me later.

By the next morning the storm had blown itself out and she awoke to a world that felt as fixed and stable and permanent as ever. She breakfasted alone; Ratcliff had left early for the hospital, and you were of course away at school. She ate a finger of buttered toast with just a smear of marmalade and drank a cup of coffee—I was avid for every detail of those hours! The alarm she had known in the night had dissipated, she told me. She felt gay and light-headed. It was a damp cold morning but the sky was clear.

Oh, but the imagination of a man in love is a florid jungle of lush, fast-growing forms of life! I had made love to your mother. Now, without yet fully grasping the essential complexity of the situation, I began to indulge in richly textured daydreams about her. She was a figure of shimmering loveliness to me. She was beauty itself, she was perfection; I lived only to see her again, and though this didn't happen for some days the waiting, at first, was less harrowing than you might imagine: my intoxication with the very *idea* that I loved her had not yet passed. So vast, so strong was this feeling, and so enamored was I of it, all else was mere detail, and beneath notice; I was in a state of bliss.

I remembered a gesture she made, a way she had of lifting her chin and at the same time glancing at me through half-closed eyes; then the smile would come, the humor of recognition, for it was a joke, we decided, that we had seen each other, and recognized each other, and in effect said to each other: I have known you all my life and here you are at last. And I wonder now—had I known that the comedy would play out as it did, would I have behaved differently? Would I have fled from her and flung myself into medicine with a passion I no longer felt, become absorbed in medicine and so hidden from her? I don't think I would. Remember Hopkins, the poem about the mind having mountains, cliffs of fall, "frightful, sheer, no-man-fathomed"? At the end there's this:

> Here! creep,
> Wretch, under a comfort serves in a whirlwind: all
> Life death does end and each day dies with sleep.

Well, no creeping for me! No comfort for me in the whirlwind! This was my feeling. Your mother and I had the same soul. We were drawn to one another by a force inexorable. It could not have happened other than it did. She'd told me that "it" had happened to her too, and this was all I needed to know; so exalted did this make me feel, her actual presence would almost have been too much; it was enough to sustain the feeling.

I see myself in the flat in Jubilee Road. I should be sleeping, but cannot. I pace up and down the faded carpet, I stop at the window and pull back the curtain and peer out—perhaps she will come to me again, perhaps I will glimpse her alighting from a cab below—? At that moment a cab does turn into Jubilee Road, and moves toward the house, and suddenly I'm convinced that *this is her*—this is her, coming to me again— but it passes without stopping and I let the curtain fall back, pace the carpet once more, pause by a sketch of a seascape at sunset. I would like to go back to the Two Eagles and order a large gin and so live again the moment when it first dawned on me that I was in love, but I cannot leave the room for fear that she will come while I am away.

I fall dispiritedly into an armchair and doze for a while. I am awoken by a knock on the door. I leap to my feet—cross the room—throw wide the door—it is Desmond Kelly, the landlady's husband. What did that friendly man see? He saw the door wrenched violently open, and standing there before him, one hand on the doorknob and the other clutching the doorframe, as though the entire structure would otherwise collapse, a wild-eyed Englishman in a dressing gown. Desmond Kelly was sympathetic. He understood the essential incoherence of the human condition. "Should I come back later, doctor?" he murmured in that soft lilt of his (he was a Cork man, and a Republican).

"What is it?" I cried.

"The wife says will you be wanting the room done out in the morning?"

"Yes!" I cried. "No letters, Desmond? No messages for me?"

"Nothing," he said, dramatically. "Not a single one, doctor."

I pushed a hand through my hair and frowned. "Thanks," I said, and turned sadly back into my room, deflated and forsaken. The lover is a comic figure, truly, but love can change its nature. It has the germ of tragedy in it.

Time passed. Not a lot of time, by normal standards, but by the clock in my heart—ages, eons, very eternities. I was desperate to see her again. I needed to nourish my love upon her being, as though my love were a ravening parasitical creature which if it could not feed upon her would feed instead upon its host, causing agony. I was in agony. Missing her was no state of tranquil melancholy, it was active, it was fiercely energetic. There came a moment when it occurred to me that she had not been in touch with me because she was dead. This idea rapidly turned to certainty and I began to grieve for her, and now —cruelest of cruel ironies—I felt that I had lost her before I had even known her—grief without even the consolation of memory! The problem was, I couldn't reach her. The idea of writing to her or telephoning her—any such move was dangerous, hadn't she told me not even to try?

And meanwhile I continued to work, functioning as best I could. An elderly prostitute called Belle Sylvester was found in an alley in a coma one night and brought into St. Basil's. It was our turn receiving from Accident and Casualty so I had to work her up. A first, cursory examination on the ward gave me no real clue as to what was wrong, though after I'd eliminated all other possible causes of coma, meningitis suggested itself. I was compelled, reluctantly, to perform a lumbar puncture.

The night sister wheeled screens round the bed then turned the unconscious Belle Sylvester on her side and bent her double, knees to head. She was a big woman, fleshy and pink. I settled myself on a chair at the bedside, frowning, uneasy— I dislike lumbar punctures, they're so damn tricky. I scrubbed the skin at the puncture site, painted it with antiseptics, then laid sterile cloths across her broad back, leaving one small patch uncovered. I picked up the big spinal needle and then, with as much delicacy as I could, inserted it. It seemed to be sliding in nicely, until suddenly—and this was what I'd been dreading—there was a horrible scraping sound—I'd hit bone. I lifted my head, looked at Sister and withdrew the needle. "It's impossible," I muttered, sitting up straight for a moment, unbuttoning my white coat and sweeping the skirts back, then hunching forward on the chair to again slide in the needle, "with her bent double like this—to aim the needle—accurately—*damn!*" Again the scraping sound—again I withdrew. I wiped my brow, took a few deep breaths, tried to shake off my fatigue. For just an instant I thought of your mother, and my penis stirred in my trousers. The problem was that if, in my search for the minute box canyon formed by the bony arches of the vertebral column, I plunged the needle in too deeply, I'd pierce a vital organ and kill the woman. I inserted the needle once more, and this time was rewarded by a pulpy feeling. "Yes," I murmured. I withdrew slowly, allowing a few drops of cerebrospinal fluid into the barrel of the syringe, then rose to my feet; the image of your mother again sprang into my mind, and for a second or two I was elsewhere.

Your father was talking about dead bodies. "This is hypostasis, gentlemen," he was saying. "Note the discoloration of the skin." He was a fat, confident man who smoked cigars to mask the smells of the cadavers with which he worked. "Begins to happen about thirty minutes after death, and takes six to eight hours till it's done. Caused by the blood gravitating downward and suffusing the lower capillaries, leaving the upper surfaces of the body pallid. Starts off pink, then rapidly darkens. Ends up purple." He gestured at the gaping cadaver before him with brisk, choppy hand movements, like a man conducting an orchestra. "Another peculiarity of the body in death, gentlemen, is the appearance of a network of bluish veins, dendritic in structure, just below the surface of the skin. Generally occurs when putrefaction is rapid." He paused and spent a moment, frowning, relighting the cigar. "Note too the shedding of the skin and the formation of adipocere. This happens when fatty tissue changes to fatty acids. You'll also see bloating as a result of methane generated by decomposition, you'll see liquefied eyeballs, you'll see blistering of the skin, you'll see dazzling changes of color, maggots, you'll even see corpses bursting open. You can never really rely on the dead to do what you expect; it all depends on temperature, moisture, insects, bacteria, oh, a host of factors."

I was down in Pathology to hear what they'd found in Eddie Bell's lungs. Your father was in the postmortem room, standing at a dissecting table in a black rubber apron, his sleeves rolled up, large hands ungloved, talking to half a dozen medical students. On the dissecting table (steel, with a central channel and a hole where body fluids were hosed down) lay the pale cadaver of Eddie himself, with his thorax split open. Also in the room was a glass-fronted cupboard containing instruments (knives, saws, bone forceps), a row of metal hooks with rubber aprons hanging from them, and a table with steel bowls for specimens, at which your father's assistant, a balding, weasel-faced fellow called Miggs, was busy with a slice of Eddie's lung. It was a small, cramped, low-ceilinged basement room with a narrow barred window at the top of one wall through which a little light was admitted, and a view of feet crossing the courtyard outside. It was cold, and stank of formalin. "Pathology makes physiology possible," your father was saying, "in the sense, gentlemen, that organic functions are revealed only when they fail." Standing there patiently, waiting till he had a moment for me, I remembered your mother's words. "Don't you wonder," she'd said, "what it is that makes men spend their lives poking through the diseased bits of dead bodies?" I could hear her voice, see her eyes, feel my lips upon her silky skin; and James, at that moment I experienced my first real spurt of antagonism toward your father.

I've often wondered—what kind of father can he have *been* to you? You were a complicated boy, sensitive, poetic—what did he do to you, this butcher of a man? It doesn't surprise me that you identified so closely with your mother, you recognized her grace and were drawn to it, and repelled (though you may never have admitted this to yourself) by your father and his death trade, everything he stood for. But if by some chance—and these were my thoughts after the evening when you'd asked me if she'd "thrown herself" at me—if your sympathies did, somehow, lie with him—then you'd see me in the blackest light. So if I were to tell you everything, as I intended to, I knew it must be done gradually, not all at once. I must slowly paint a picture of your parents' marriage, a portrait which, if subtle enough, and accurate enough, would lead you irresistibly to an understanding of your mother's unhappiness—the causes of it—and my own effort, ultimately unsuccessful, to relieve it, and offer her the life of hope and joy she deserved, and from which your father blocked her. This as I say was my intention, and if I haven't fulfilled it the fault lies not with me, but somewhere in the tangled chain of circumstance and accident that has brought us here, now.

The tangled chain. I lift my head. My eyes are streaming tears. Hangars at the edge of the airfield, long low structures growing indistinct as the light begins to go. Figures moving across the grass toward us, waving their arms; faint shouts reach my ears. Over on the far side the ack-ack gun, the dispersal hut, behind them trees, a church spire, all smudged against the evening sky. Hard at times to believe there's a war on, up here on the Downs, among these grassy rolling hills where sheep, and old stone walls, and the odd copse of oak and elm are the features of the country: this is farmland, grazing land . . .

In retrospect the whole sequence of events—all that's happened since I first began to practice medicine down here—it all seems merely a sort of prelude to your arrival. As though I was sent here so as to witness—what, exactly? Was it just a rare and curious medical phenomenon, what started happening to your body, entirely explicable in scientific terms? Or something much stranger, more glorious? Even now I waver. Even now I cannot be sure. What I believe in the morning I doubt at night. What I'm sure of at night is fantastic in the morning. As is the idea that I was *sent here*. I am a doctor, finally, but must that necessarily preclude a belief in fate? In some higher plan? Some design? At times I'm inclined to think not. At times I'm inclined to doubt the tangled chain, the random weave of circumstance and accident. At times I'm inclined to believe that the whole point and meaning of my life has been to lead me to *this precise moment*—here—with you—at twilight—in the shadow of a blazing Spitfire.

It was the spring of '39. I believed I was recovering. My first dreadful winter in Elgin had passed, the weather was improving, and I tried to get out of the house as often as I could to walk on the beach and breathe the good sea air. That spring I discovered a method of managing the wooden staircase down the cliff that Spike seemingly could tolerate. It involved leading with the good leg, descending sideways, and making frequent stops. It was time-consuming, tiring, and uncomfortable, but it was worth it: the beach was usually deserted in the early evening, and I could ramble along at my leisure, poking with my stick at shells and seaweed and odd bits of fishing gear that had washed up with the afternoon tide. There was a flat rock I liked to sit on to smoke a cigarette and watch the sun go down, and stretch out the bad leg and give Spike a rest, and think about the day, and watch the shadows lengthen and the sea grow dark, as the crags and hollows of the cliff face behind me turned black in the twilight. I wouldn't go back the way I'd come, but by a path that ascended fairly gently to the road, then up the road to the top of the cliffs and so to Elgin.

Though Spike would make me pay for my exertions. The evening would find me in severe pain in the gloom of the surgery. I'd have at hand a steel bowl, kidney-shaped, in which lay my big hypodermic needle; and an ampoule of morphia. I'd tap it smartly then snap off the top. Draw up the fluid into the syringe—a squirt or two to expel the air— and from the lifted needle droplets fountain in the twilight. With my jacket draped over my shoulders I perch there on the edge of my desk and roll up my sleeve, and tie the rubber tourniquet till the veins of my inner arm bulge against the skin. A quick swab, fist clenched tight, then the needle slides in and the plunger is carefully depressed. After a moment or two the syringe clatters back into its bowl and the tourniquet is tossed onto the desk. Still with my sleeve rolled up, still with my jacket draped about my shoulders, I make my slow way upstairs. Somewhere in the house a clock faintly chimes the half hour; otherwise all is still.

I remember there was one evening that spring that I found myself dressing for a dinner party being thrown by Hugh Fig and his wife. I had no desire to attend the thing, but saw no way of getting out of it—and I wonder now, *why* must it all cling to memory, every damn detail—why can't I *forget?* Because, I suppose, this was the first dinner party I'd attended since the Cushings', and so completely had my heart and mind been colonized by memories of your mother there was little in the world that didn't trigger pain. I remember opening my wardrobe and taking out my dinner jacket and becoming acutely aware of the last time I'd worn it—but what a different man gazed back at me now from the mirror in the wardrobe door! I was in my vest and trousers, my braces hanging down my thighs, my stick hooked on the chair nearby, and what a

skinny specimen I'd become, I thought, as I regarded the
ravaged, wild-haired, too-large head atop the bony narrow
shoulders and the sunken hairless chest; and I remembered
the days before Spike when I was not thin but wiry, when
hard work maintained a distinct musculature of my small-
boned frame, when your mother, at least, despite my ill-
proportion, had seemed to like the look of me. Hard to imagine anyone liking the look of me now, I reflected. Now I
looked puny. I looked like a shrimp, a crested shrimp.

But oh, no maundering tonight, Spike had been silenced
and even as I started dressing I began to feel expansive. I
slipped on my dress shirt, and buttoned it, and as my fingers
deftly attached with studs the collar and cuffs I saw the familiar
transformation begin, the familiar magic that this ritual never
fails to perform, the metamorphosis of a shrimp into a man
in evening dress. I pulled on the trousers and the patent
leather shoes and tied the black bow tie. Cummerbund? I
thought not, from a conviction that the evening's company
would have scant appreciation for good tailoring. A last glance
at myself in profile in the mirror, and what was that lovely
thing of Max's?—"all delicate spirits assume an oblique attitude toward life."

Some minutes later I heaved myself in behind the wheel
of the Humber and turned out of the drive onto the coast
road. The sun had set, and the sight of the sea fired my senses
with exhilaration: it was a skin of rippled black satin, with the
moonlight washing over it like golden oil. As I drove I wound
down the window and listened to its calm voice, its subtle
symphony, the slur and hiss as it rolled and murmured and
slapped at the rocks beneath the cliffs. On the other side of
Griffin Head I pulled into the driveway of the Figs' villa.

Out of the car, up to the front door, barely had I rung the
bell than a housemaid opened the door and then Hugh Fig
hove up behind her, welcomed me warmly, and led me across
the hall. Great big lanky man, like a heron. I liked him.

"What's your poison, doctor?" he said. What did Barbey say about the British? "A people of the north, lymphatic and pale, like their mother the sea, but loving to heat their blood at the flame of alcohol." Lovely.

"Gin and tonic, if I may."

There were three or four people in the drawing room. Hugh introduced me first to his wife, Jean, a tense woman of about forty with a slightly yellowish discoloration of the skin that suggested a liver complaint of some kind. As we shook hands I wondered idly what her urine looked like. The other couple were the Piker-Smiths, Harold and Vera. The name rang a bell. He was a doctor, a dull man with a practice in Wimbledon. She was tall and thin, had teeth like a horse, and gushed at me with enormous volubility. She shook my hand powerfully and bent toward me like a tree bowed by the wind. "Dr. Haggard!" she cried. "I've so been longing to meet you! I think we have people in common." It then came back to me that her husband had been attached to St. Basil's. "Fanny Vaughan—don't you know Fanny?"

I did not respond—I could not respond! A moistness sprang to my eyes. She had hit the mark with her very first arrow. That one remark did for me for the rest of the evening.

I arrived back at Elgin shortly after ten-thirty and immediately made for the surgery. Then I went upstairs to the back bedroom, hung up my dinner jacket, untied my bow tie and unfastened my collar. I went to the window. The first sensation was one of profound relief: I had escaped those dreadful people, and as I stood there gazing at the moonlit sea the terrible sense of loss and yearning that had been aroused by Vera Piker-Smith's question softened. I leaned against the window frame, shifted my weight onto my good leg, laid my head against the windowpane and with my right hand gently thumped the wall a number of times as a sort of dry, tormented, sobbing noise came from my throat. Oh God. When

was it that I had become such a fool of love? It had been at
that funeral, the seed had been sown that day, that's when it
had started to grow, down in the dark soil of my heart, and
me all unsuspecting until it burst forth, sturdy and vigorous
in its maturity—oh _God!_ I lifted my head, shook it briskly
and blew the air out of my lungs like a walrus. The wind had
died, the moon was hidden behind a patch of black cloud;
the sky was alive with stars. I could stay in the house not a
moment longer. I seized up my dinner jacket from the back
of the chair, and my stick, and with as much haste as I could
manage I clattered down the stairs and out through the back
door onto the path that led through the gate at the bottom of
the garden to the edge of the cliff and the staircase down to
the beach. I had never attempted it at night, it was only in
the last week or two that I'd discovered that Spike could in
fact manage the descent at all, but in my desperation to get
out, get _away_, get down to the water, to be anywhere but
cooped up in Elgin with my damn memories, my damn _feel-
ings_—it didn't occur to me that descending the staircase at
midnight would offer any more of a problem than it did at
dusk.

And at first it didn't. Still in a state almost of panic I hauled
Spike down the first dozen steps before pausing to catch my
breath. I was suddenly and intensely conscious of the darkness, first, and second, of the sound of the sea crashing onto
the beach far below me, and that its black and heaving surface,
the gleaming rocks, the shelf of pebbles and the stretch of
hard damp sand, all of it was but dimly discernible by starlight
alone. But what came to me then even more vividly was the
powerful sense of having entered an unknown and possibly
dangerous region, the cliff face so familiar to me by daylight
now a black mass of shadow into which my excited mind began
immediately and in spite of myself to project its terrors. For
the first time the cliff face felt alive, alien, hostile—benev-
olent watchers by day, these bulwarks, now they were mon-

sters, living gargoyles, rearing and looming for a thousand years, and it seemed to me that by leaving the top of the cliff and beginning this descent I had abandoned all light and security and given myself over to—what? The dark? The night? I laughed aloud, but the thin sound of it was quickly swallowed, leaving me as desolate as before. I began once more to descend.

Oh what are you doing? I asked myself. Isn't there something ridiculous about all this—you feed your obsession with the woman with morphia until you're unable to think of anything else, you can't sleep, you can't even stay in the house— as though Elgin were your own head, your own mind—as though by escaping Elgin you can escape the thoughts and feelings and memories that roil and turn endlessly, endlessly *in* that mind—it's not romantic at all! But down I went anyway, sideways, like a crab, good leg first, then Spike, then the stick, good leg, Spike, stick, and then I began actually to savor the terror that this plunge into a black unknown aroused in me. Was I mad, I wondered, voluntarily to push myself further and further into the darkness—my vulnerability increased with each step I took. But vulnerability to what?

There are close to a hundred stairs in that steep staircase, divided into nine unequal flights, each flight following a particular tack down the cliff then changing direction as the face of the cliff dictates, a short platform facilitating each change of tack so the structure seems to zigzag down, a fragile business of sticks and nails clinging to the great broad bulk of the cliff like a centipede. I did not pause again until I was halfway down; I turned to see how far I'd come, and the top of the staircase, a few uprights and a length of railing, stood out sharply over the lip of the cliff against the starry sky. Then I looked down: still the moon was hidden in a bank of heavy cloud, and the sea, the beach, all was black, though a faint gleam of frothing showed around the humped black rocks where the tide crashed against them and rolled hissing up the

sand. A few minutes later I was painfully clambering off the
staircase and scrambling down the last few yards of a boulder-
strewn gully and onto the beach.

The cliffs made of this stretch of beach a crescent-shaped
cove, and there was a powerful sense, with the sheer walls
behind me, and the tide hissing across the sand, of being
embosomed in a small dark watery pocket of the night. I'd
turned up my collar and hunched my shoulders against the
wind, my one hand gripping my stick, banging it into the
pebbles with every forward step, and the other hand stuffed
in my pocket clenching and unclenching to the steady rhythm
of the jabs of protest coming from Spike, and the pulse of the
sea, and the ebb and flow of my own emotions; and as I raged
along I suddenly saw my relationship with your mother for
what it was—not, as your father would have it, the infatuation
of a foolish and deluded young man with a sophisticated older
woman, not that at all, nothing could be further from the
truth. The reality of our relationship could never be understood in such terms, as your father thought, no, in a condition
of romantic love it is the *soul* that speaks, it is a discourse of
soul with soul, and all else is behavior, even the sex. For what
is sex after all but a cleaving together and a fusion? It is the
making of the two into the one, the recovery of a *lost unity*,
and this is what I saw that night, that she and I were—are—
two parts of a single whole. This of course is no new idea,
this is not original with me, it is a Platonic idea, it arises in
the very dawn of our civilization: I am a fragment, a broken
thing; I am incomplete and unfinished. Blindly I groped my
way through the world, seeking, though I did not know it,
for that which would complete me. She completed me, but
I lost her. And having known fusion and wholeness it became
impossible to live without it—I'd rather *never have known* that
such a condition was possible.

And then I thought: so what can I hope for now? There is
only the one: for I love not out of need but from the recog-

nition of the profound spiritual communion I share—with her! Only with her! This is why I left London and why, even though I was still a relatively young man when I did so, her loss marked in a sense the end of my life. But I chose to go on; I chose to follow my calling, I chose to serve, and the full weight of that decision was borne home to me that night, as I turned at last, and retraced my steps, and struggled painfully back up the staircase from the beach. For the steps that lay before me, each of them demanding that Spike be lifted, howling, and set down, lifted and set down, those steps were like the days that remained to me, each one of them bringing its demands, its labor, its pain—and no sweetness in recompense, no peace, no love, no rest, no grace. No grace—until, that is, you came.

That night on the stairs I saw a toiling unto death. And I saw that all I had to relieve the burden of that toiling were a few weak dim shadows of love: poetry, I mean, and music, for it is the nature of art to be a shadow or echo of love, an attempt to represent love, but an attempt doomed to produce only melancholy, for it carries within itself the lack or loss of that to which it aspires, which as I say is love. And that is all the solace that remains to me—this I realized, climbing back up to Elgin that night—all I have are the husks and shadows of love, I who once possessed the thing itself.

And I do do my work, I am treating my patients, I am taking morning surgery each day, and making my house calls in the afternoon. Whatever I may have lost, and I have lost much, I have not lost this, my commitment to service, to duty. I do my work, I read the poets, and I watch the changing arc of the sun in the sky as spring turns into summer, and the evening shadows thicken, and you, dear boy, lie dying in my arms—

That night marked an important change in my thinking about your mother. After that night I no longer attempted to suppress my memories, nor the feelings that were inevitably excited by their arousal. I understood that our love affair would influence me profoundly—define me probably—for the rest of my life, and this being so, I chose, freely, not to forget. I would not, I decided, allow the memory to atrophy, to wither and fade, I would keep it fresh, I would nurture it, make of it an object of worship and construct an altar in my heart where I could perform, nightly, my devotions. I'd realized you see that I was one of those rare men who, having loved, come to understand love as the most significant spiritual activity a man can undertake. Love, for me, is not ephemeral, it is not a transient emotion, a passing state, a passage or flight into madness or ecstasy; I see it, rather, as an exalted or even *sacred* condition, a condition in which all the highest and best of human faculties are exercised. Your mother had said to me the night we met that passion was not a sickness, not a disease, but was, rather, the best we were capable of, civilized human beings. Ironically, it was I who came to embrace the idea, while she—

It was hard, nonetheless, in the days following the Figs' dinner party to cope with the memories that now intruded constantly into my thoughts. I remembered her clothes, her conversation, the way she ate, drank, laughed—it all came bubbling back into consciousness at random moments and despite this decision I'd made it never failed to distress me. One morning I was examining an old man with a lung condition, bending over my patient with a stethoscope, when suddenly I saw your mother's wrist—a slender, rather bony wrist, a delicate stem, otherwise unremarkable, but it was stamped indelibly in the fabric of my memory and was enough to make me leave the room and spend a minute or two mastering the sudden overwhelming movement of grief within myself. At times like this I lost faith: why couldn't I abandon her, I wondered? After all I'd suffered, why hang on like this? I could so easily call up the negative: ponder the hurts I'd suffered directly or indirectly through her; stir up a good smoky blaze of resentment and so attempt to find relief in the fact that it was over, that I had escaped the constant turmoil of violent feeling she aroused in me—why not do it, I asked myself, why not vilify the woman, know her as the source and agent of all the misery I had gone through in the last months? Hating her, I thought, would be easier than continuing to love her like this.

But I couldn't do it. I tried, but I couldn't. Why not? Why not just summon her image and hold it up to a distorting mirror—no beauty is so flawless that from a certain angle, in a certain light, it cannot be rendered grotesque, and the power to effect such a transformation resides always with the observer—why not? But I couldn't spoil her; the horror of spoiling was, to me, more terrible even than the daily anguish of missing her, missing her so acutely and with such convulsive unhappiness that at times I felt death would be preferable: no, the horror of spoiling exceeded the pain. The pain I could endure, I *would* endure, but to spoil her, to blacken her, to violate her image in my heart—this I could not do. Why not? Because—and here I sighed, recognizing the exquisitely mordant irony of it all—because I loved her. And that would never change.

No, that would never change—that never *has* changed, as you better than anyone can confirm. How could I otherwise have welcomed you with the warmth I did, were there any trace of bitterness or anger in my heart? Or worse, had I forgotten her, or grown indifferent? I loved not *what* she was, but *that* she was. You see, inasmuch as everything your mother had ever touched was for me impregnated with power (the fly-in-glass was then, and still is, at all times in my right-hand trouser pocket) then how much greater by extension the power of the being whom she had not merely touched but created?

Though what she created they have now destroyed.

·   ·   ·

Poor darling boy. Poor *ruined* boy, with the light of Heaven in your dying eyes—sleep. So what was I to tell you—that it was *Ratcliff's* fault? No, that would be too much, too soon, I decided. Too much truth. Go slow, I told myself. Find out what the boy is made of. What he can take. More than ever it was vitally important to me that you understand, for in some curious way I felt that I owed it to *her* that despite all you had to deal with, despite having to carry the secret of your disease—you should have the truth; and that if I told you the kind of woman she was then you, like me, could carry her flame and her spirit forward, and thus she would never die, not truly die. Not an ignoble impulse, I think? Though sadly, you had no opportunity to grasp what it was I was trying to tell you before you came flaming from the sky like a dying god and now I shall be left, again, to be the sole witness and carrier, not only of herself but of you also, or rather of her *in* you, fused in you.

A vast aeroplane hangar with a bowed roof of corrugated tin and massive sliding doors painted blue—this was the first thing one saw, coming up to the station; and in its shadow was the pilots' mess. In time I came to know it well, that one-story prefabricated structure with its few functional armchairs, bare wooden floor, its scattering of tables and a bar that ran the length of one wall, hanging above it like a trophy the propeller from some unlucky German bomber. At the other end of this long narrow room stood a battered upright piano, and I remember going past one day on my way to the sick bay and being startled to hear, drifting in the morning air and mixing incongruously with the smells and sounds of aeroplanes, the melancholy notes of a favorite Chopin nocturne. Looking in at the window I saw a young pilot called Johnny Hart sitting at that battered piano, a cigarette between his lips, and last night's beer glasses still on top. I was rather moved.

But the first evening I was invited up to the mess it was not Chopin that was being banged out on that old upright, far from it—the pilots were having a party, a party to which you, to my delight, had invited me. I'd been concerned, I remember, about your relations with the other pilots, about how a complicated, sensitive boy like yourself was treated by those rough hearty men. I needn't have worried. Squadron spirit was unlike that of any other tight-bonded community of men I'd ever known or been part of. For beneath the raucous shouts of laughter, and the incessant pounding of the piano, beneath it all I discerned a thread of intense mutual devotion, an inarticulate intimacy, born, I guessed, of constant shared danger and the proximity of sudden violent death—a form of *love,* though of course I would never have said such a thing to any of you, you'd have been embarrassed and scornful at the very thought of it.

You were at the bar when I came in. You saw me at the door and immediately came over to greet me. "Hello doctor," you said warmly, taking me by the elbow, "come over and have a drink with B Flight." You introduced me to three or four pilots, clean, brisk, affable young men smoking pipes and drinking beer, standing in the familiar RAF stance, legs apart, hands plunged deep in the side pockets of your tunics. I was given a large gin and asked a few questions, but conversation soon veered round to aeroplanes, and crashes, and senior offices, and I listened with pleasure as the RAF slang rolled off your tongues—your kites and prangs, your pieces of nice, your swank, your Spits, your curtains. It was clear to me that you were different from the other men; that evening I saw that they sensed it too, and that it provoked in them a certain deference toward you, a certain gallantry, as though they understood that this slim youth was special. You never joined the group singing at the piano, you preferred to stand with the pipe-smoking talkers at the bar, narrow-shouldered and slim-hipped, a small smile on your lips and one of the other young men at all times in attendance by your side, murmuring remarks, lighting your cigarettes—and it was hard for me not to think of some other evening, some other room, and the same small figure in a black fur coat, glancing at me with a lazy smile through half-closed eyes—

For she had come again, as I knew she would, and she had come bearing gifts—a volume of poetry and a bottle of gin. Poetry was to become one of our shared passions; I introduced your mother to the lovely lines

Ay, in the very temple of Delight
Veil'd Melancholy has her sovran shrine . . .

She loved the ode, and often had me read it to her. It was quite unfashionable, then, to like Romantics, but we didn't care. But yes: at last she'd come. I had been growing more frantic with each day that passed, each day with no sight of her, no word from her, I was going mad; imagine my relief when I got her note telling me when I could expect her. I stood at my window gazing down into Jubilee Road with mounting impatience; eventually I saw a taxi pull up outside the house, saw the door swing open, saw a slender black oxford, a stockinged calf, the hem of a skirt, the woman herself. I was down the stairs and at the front door before she could ring the bell and rouse Desmond Kelly from the back of the house. She was just ascending the steps, carefully, for it was icy out, with one gloved hand on the railing and the other clutching her parcels to the breast of her fur. Her hat was an elegant affair with a narrow brim that swept forward low over one eye. She lifted her face to me; her skin was whiter than ever in the cold air, her eyes slightly damp, very blue, and sparkling. "Hello," she said; we embraced in the hallway, rather gently, as though careful of damaging one another.

She ascended first, and for the briefest sliver of time a

strange shadow fell across my soul. Lambs to the slaughter: the phrase sprang into my mind from nowhere, as I climbed the staircase behind her, though of course I did not voice it. In my room she made straight for the gas fire and stood there with her back to it, pulling off her gloves. I hovered. "What can I give you?" I began.

"Well," she said, "first take these"—she handed me the parcels—"and now you can hang up my coat, though on second thought it's rather reckless of me to surrender it. I'll keep it on for the moment." That *smile!* "The book and the bottle are for you."

I then had business with book and bottle. "It's been perfectly beastly," she began; "thank you darling," as I gave her her gin. She was sitting in an armchair now, her legs crossed, one ankle pulled in close to the other, in a beautiful dove-gray suit cut on tailored, mannish lines, with broad shoulders and a straight skirt, and the big black fur of course, I could never get that bloody room warm enough for her!—when after only a moment she stood up and came across to my chair, and leaning forward cupped my face in her hands and stared a long, searching moment into my eyes, and told me she was sorry I'd been miserable, she never ever wanted to make me miserable again, though she thought she probably would.

I didn't know what she meant.

"Oh darling. Use your imagination."

The moment passed, she sat down again and began talking. "I was too distraught for words," she said, as I leaned across to light her cigarette, and she blew smoke at the ceiling. She knew we had to take great care, for Ratcliff must never find out, but it made her simply wild not to be able to see me, her clever, noble, handsome lover with the terribly difficult decision to make about his career. "I've been thinking about it," she said, "and I don't think you should go into surgery. I know surgeons. They lose sight of what matters. Their patients are unconscious when they do their real work. You're so good with people, I think you'll be much more use in general medicine."

"Good with people?" It had never occurred to me that I was good with people.

"Good with me. Darling, it's so *cold* in here!"

I was moved, deeply, that she would think about me and my problems. "I know it is," I said, "I'm afraid there's nothing I can do to get it any warmer. Would you like to go somewhere else?"

"Oh?" She stood up and wandered to my bookshelves, touched the spines of this and that. I was standing by the fire now with one hand in my pocket, the other gripping my gin My heart was racing. "I've found a nice little pub," I said. "Very quiet."

She moved back to the fire. "You look like a schoolmaster," she murmured. She took the gin from me and put it on the mantelpiece, then put her arms around me. She pressed herself gently against me. I closed my eyes. One hand at the small of her back—the other in the silky-soft hair at the back of her neck—her perfume in my nostrils. She pushed her thigh between mine. "What pub?" she breathed into my ear.

"The Two Eagles," I whispered, moving my hand up and down her back, under the jacket of her suit, feeling how soft the silk of her blouse was, and how soft the skin beneath. "It's warm too."

"And quiet?"

"Always empty."

"No one goes there?"

"Only me."

"It'll be our pub."

Our lips touched. She kissed me. It was the softest kiss imaginable. I was already deeply aroused. I felt a dampness in my underpants. She pulled gently free of me. My heart rate was high, my respiration shallow. I was very happy indeed in a very foolish way. All I wanted was to keep holding her, forever. That would be enough. I told her so. "Shall we go to bed?" she whispered.

Afterwards she sat in the armchair in front of the fire and I sat on the floor with my head on her knee. Still we sustained that impossibly exquisite tension—how rare it is, and how sweet! She felt it too, she told me; she thought: this is a gift, where did it come from? "I remembered your eyes being green," I said.

"They go blue in the cold," she said, and we laughed! How we laughed! It wasn't the least bit funny, but such was our happiness that laughter was at least an outlet. Then we drank more gin; it made no difference; we were already drunk. "Did you look at your book?" she said. It was Keats. I opened it at random. "She cannot fade, though thou hast not thy bliss," I read, "For ever wilt thou love, and she be fair." It sobered us a little. I lifted my eyes from the book and gazed at her; she turned her head aside.

She told me later what happened when she got home that evening. In the cab, she said, she sat powdering her face and feeling wicked and guilty, but at the same time she was aware of other, stronger emotions, emotions that were associated with me, my idealism, my love. They flourished quietly, she said, in the darkness of her heart, but sitting in a cold cab on the way home to Plantagenet Gardens and Ratcliff—she was miserable.

But then, she said, her mood changed. All at once she realized she need not feel so terribly maudlin about it all. Some little flicker of domestic cruelty, or indifference, from Ratcliff—the mere memory of such a flicker, she said, a pin-prick, no more, of marital distaste such as she had felt a thousand times—that had been stimulus enough, given the delicacy of her moral and emotional condition at this point; I forget precisely what it was. Whatever it was, she thought again of me, and the anxiety vanished. It all comes of un-derstanding renunciation, she said—how easy it is to renounce one's pleasure, but how resilient, compared to the tedium of self-mortification, is its memory. She would banish her guilt, she said; Christmas was coming, you would be home, it was hardly the time to have the specter of adultery hovering about the place.

It was with this figure uppermost in her mind—the hovering specter of adultery—that she paid off the cab and let herself into the house. The light was on in Ratcliff's study. "That you?" he called as she closed the front door softly behind her.

She stood before the mirror in the hall, taking off her hat. "Yes it is," she called back.

"Come in and have a nightcap."

Oh God. She'd dreaded this. He sounded genial. She'd hoped to be able to slip quietly up to her room, and nine nights out of ten this would have presented no problem; nine nights out of ten the study door would be closed, with him wrapped in his precious solitude like a larva in a cocoon. Tonight of all nights he was genial. All too easy for me to reconstruct what followed; your mother talked to me at length about Ratcliff, for I was always intensely curious to know what went on between them. She stood in the doorway with her hand to her mouth, covering a false yawn. "No nightcap for me, Ratcliff," she said, "I'm exhausted."

"Come in for a moment," he said. "I want to talk to you." A flicker of alarm—about *what?* He was in his leather armchair, a scotch in a cut crystal glass at his elbow, the standard lamp directed onto the book in his hand. He was in his gray velvet smoking jacket and Moroccan slippers.

She went in. She wandered along his bookshelves, keeping her back to him. She pulled out a volume at random and idly turned the pages. The carpet was thick beneath her feet, the lighting warm, the traces of an after-dinner cigar still faintly lingering. "How is Brenda?"

"Much as usual."

"Pleasant evening?"

"Oh fine. Ladies' night out, you know." She turned to face him, still with the book in her hand. "We talk about our husbands, analyze their manly qualities."

He frowned. Oh why do this, she thought, why provoke him? This is what happens in marriage, she told me—one snipes away constantly, resentment never sleeps. "I wanted to talk to you about James," said Ratcliff. "I suppose it can wait till the morning."

She heard the touch of chill in his voice. "I'm sorry, dear, I didn't mean to be beastly. I'm tired, I think I'll go up."

He nodded. She put down the book, crossed the room and kissed his forehead. "Sorry," she murmured, and came behind his chair and began gently to massage his temples.

"Ah," he said, "that is exquisite."

"Headache?"

"Since about two this afternoon. Nothing works on them anymore."

She continued to massage his temples, his forehead, the nape of his neck. He had grown fat in recent years; her fingers kneaded a thick roll of flesh at his collar. She often told me how distasteful she found it to have to touch him. He groaned with pleasure. "Nothing gives me relief, but you can.'"

"Poor thing. You work too hard." It was a familiar conversation.

"I know. That is good, my darling." She felt the knotted muscles beneath the soft fat, felt them slacken as she worked out the tension with her fingers. "I'll come to you later, may I?" he said quietly.

"I don't think so tonight. I'm very tired."

"As you wish." Again that sudden chill; that *ice*.

"Goodnight Ratcliff," she said. It was typical, she told me, that his tenderness, so rarely aroused, should vanish with such abruptness if he sensed the slightest rebuff. But he made no effort, he hadn't for years. He was fat, and he always smelled of formalin. It was a smell that made her think of pathology labs, and cadavers. He came to her smelling of death, she said, cigars, whiskey and death. She went upstairs to her room and sat at her dressing table. She opened a jar of cleansing cream and began gently working it into her skin with the tips of her fingers. She felt calm and sad and now her conscience didn't trouble her in the slightest.

All this flickered through my mind in the few moments I stood at the bar of the mess half listening to a fighter pilot tell a tale of high adventure in the sky—and at the same time watching your face. Oh, but you loved being among them, this was clear, you reveled, in your quiet way, in the company of these dashing, handsome, brave young men, you took a keen delight in all the robust, physically affectionate conviviality they displayed though without, somehow, ever fully participating in it—you looked on, for instance, when, quite late in the evening, the squadron formed a human crocodile that then crawled about the floor snapping at the skirts and trousers of the visitors. It seemed clear to me that you were a strange one, temperamentally, for a fighter pilot—there was an aggressively competitive streak in almost all the pilots I met at the station that you seemed to lack, and naturally I wondered what happened when you climbed into the cockpit, if it manifested there. It was only later that I understood that you lacked it almost entirely, that aggressive drive, and that it was probably in order to compensate for that lack, and to prove to yourself you were a proper man, that you'd become a fighter pilot in the first place.

During the course of the evening I was introduced to the station medical officer, and the next morning I drove up the hill and offered him my assistance, an offer which he gratefully accepted. Many of my older patients had died by this time, others had been called up, and I had time on my hands; also, during the extended period of despair I had gone through in the autumn and winter I had not perhaps been as attentive to the practice as I might have been, and it was not flourishing. But now my spirits were lifting, and I was eager to work once more. I remember that I parked outside the sick bay, but before going in I stood a moment at the edge of the airfield, leaning on my stick, and gazed across the grass at the squadron sprawled in deck chairs by the dispersal hut on the far side. It was a warm clear day, the sky was deep blue with just a few high plump pillowy clouds, and you looked the very picture of languid nonchalance, there in your deck chairs, dozing in the sunshine. Sunlight glinted on the Perspex cockpit hoods of the Spitfires lined up wingtip to wingtip on the grass nearby, but even as I watched you a head appeared out of the window of the dispersal hut, there came a single shouted command— and you scrambled. Now there was nothing languid about you at all! You went sprinting across the grass (exhilarating sight!), buckling parachute harnesses over flapping leather jackets, your trousers tucked into heavy flight boots, on your heads close-fitting leather helmets, the chin straps undone, the goggles on top, and within seconds you were clambering into your cockpits and gunning your engines. Then one by one you bumped across the grass, flames leaping from your exhaust, and within a few seconds you were airborne, in formation, and rapidly climbing!

As I was leaving the station an hour later I saw a solitary Spitfire come in to land, and watched the pilot haul himself out of the cockpit and tramp silently across the grass, having perhaps witnessed (I imagined) a man going down in flames who an hour ago was playing chess with him. Curious thing, that you should be stationed in the hills above this most moribund of seaside towns, your presence, I remember, seemed to me at times like a whisper of dark necromancy, as though spirit were somehow being breathed into a corpse.

Not surprisingly my dealings with your father in the hospital became increasingly uncomfortable. I didn't like to condemn the man out of hand, but it was hard, in light of what your mother told me about what went on in Plantagenet Gardens, not to bear real animus toward him. One day shortly after Belle Sylvester died (she never came out of her coma) I was down in Pathology watching Miggs do a craniotomy on the woman. After dissecting the scalp, and folding back the flaps of skin, he sawed round the exposed skull and cracked it off with a head chisel. How he enjoyed his work, gruesome little man! He grinned at me in his weaselly way when the crack came. "Like a walnut, eh?" he murmured. He lifted it off with a flourish. Underneath I could clearly see that the dura was covered with a sugary-looking fibrinous exudate, and I knew my diagnosis was correct. Meningitis. Nothing I could have done.

Leaving the postmortem room I almost collided with Ratcliff, also on his way upstairs, wearing a black rubber apron under a starched white coat flapping open. He had a cigar between his teeth and his manner was brisk. "Ah, Dr. Haggard," he said. "Get any joy from the woman?"

For an appalled instant I misunderstood him, but it was my patient he meant. "Much as I expected, doctor," I said. I attempted to give the impression of being in a great hurry, which indeed I was. "Don't rush," he said, "we'll walk up together. This is a teaching hospital, we're an intellectual community, we should always make time to talk. You know," he said, as we made our way along the windowless corridors of the hospital basement, past the incinerator room, beneath lagged pipes that wheezed and seeped, "a lot of you people upstairs have strange opinions of what goes on down here. No, you needn't be polite, I know what gets said. But let me tell you what the great Romberg Snoddie told me, many years ago. It's the *pathos* that conditions the *logos*, do you see what I mean?"

Pathos and *logos?* Suffering and science? Strange way he had with small talk, your father. I was aware of the smell of formalin—the smell of death!—as I murmured something, I forget quite what, some half-remembered scrap of morbid anatomy.

"Precisely. Now answer me this: what is medicine?"

We were climbing the steep stone staircase that ascended by two stages to the ground floor. The wooden handrail was attached to the wall with brass fixtures; it had been worn smooth by generations of doctors and lab assistants and medical archivists and janitors. What is medicine? I should have been in theaters five minutes ago; Vincent Cushing became furious if he was kept waiting. You father didn't wait for my answer.

"Science of life," he said, as we paused on the landing halfway up for him to relight his cigar. "But life, doctor, can only create a science of itself by means of dysfunction and pain."

"Ah," I said. This glee with which he had buttonholed me—did he, it suddenly occurred to me, *suspect* something? My unease intensified.

"I analyze the dysfunction," he said, "you deal with the pain. Am I right?"

"I suppose so."

"Complementary activities. Therapeutics can only arise on the basis of pathology, I daresay you've heard that before."

"Yes indeed, Dr. Vaughan."

"Don't patronize me, Dr. Haggard."

This came out very sharply indeed. I stopped and turned, as your father shouted with brief laughter and clapped me on the shoulder. "Don't lose sight of the *pathos*, doctor," he cried, and strode away across the lobby.

Later, when I was having lunch with McGuinness in the junior common room, I mentioned what your father had said. "Odd birds, pathologists," said McGuinness, "very odd indeed. Never met one I liked. Now what sort of a doctor wants to hang around the tombs all day? In some cultures they keep

the corpse in the house till it rots. I think there's something
primitive makes a man go into pathology. I pity the wife."
    "Oh?"
    "Imagine living with Ratty Vaughan."
    Things were quiet on the ward that day, and I had leisure
to reflect on McGuinness's words. What was it, after all, that
inspired a physician to devote his career to cadavers rather
than living human beings? A deficiency in the emotional
sphere, without doubt. I began then to see your father's behavior at home in a much clearer light. He was a senior pathologist, but he was also an emotional primitive; and the idea
that such a man should be married to an exquisite, delicate
woman like your mother—I found it hard to contemplate, it
made me so angry. It still does. For you see, I believe he
didn't merely destroy her chance to be happy, I believe he
destroyed yours too.

Was it pressure from Ratcliff I wondered that led you to join
the RAF and become a fighter pilot? He was so utterly and
aggressively male, with his leather aprons and his booming
voice and his big cigars, it was not difficult to imagine him
imposing his own particular twisted ideal of masculinity on
his son. At times you seemed so young, practically a school-
boy, and I was impressed—I was *awed*, rather—to think of
the work you did in the sky each day. I'd look at that fresh
boyish face, the clear eyes with their thin dark brows con-
verging to a delicate arrowpoint at the top of that small straight
nose, and around your red lips no sign yet of the weary irony
that inevitably comes to stamp the English face—you should
have had no more to think about than Latin prep and cricket
bats and the spirit of the Upper Sixth! No, not hard to imagine
Ratcliff wanting to make a "proper" man of you, and you
succumbing, giving yourself over to it with gusto, in fact,
afraid of admitting to him and perhaps even to yourself just
how deeply unsuited you were by nature for the work of a

Spitfire pilot. Though I never doubted your love of flight—
that was always clear to me, the way your eyes lit up when
you talked about it. Once you told me that to be earthbound
was in a way to be blind, so I asked you if you thought *I* was
blind.

You paused here. "No, I don't think you are," you said.
"You're not caught up with petty things. You have an imagination. I think you're a pilot in spirit."

"I'm flattered."

You blushed. "Sorry, was that impertinent?"

"No, dear boy," I cried, "it was not! I'm delighted you
should think me a pilot in spirit—I'm afraid I feel like a
crippled shrimp much of the time."

I meant it, too; I treasured the compliment, I kept it close,
like the fly-in-glass your mother gave me for Christmas . . .

. . . the Christmas of 1937, when we were deeply in
love . . . but forced by circumstance to keep our love out of
sight, and to meet always in quiet places, where we wouldn't
be known—love in the shadows. I remember describing to
your mother my strange, uneasy encounter with your father
on the stairs in St. Basil's, and I remember that she'd smiled.
"That sounds like Ratcliff," she said, and I was bewildered
by the warmth that accompanied her words—was it affection?
Nothing, surely, as strong as that. Familiarity, yes. Boredom,
scorn? So hard to know. Your parents had been married for
seventeen years, and I'm aware that complex patterns of feeling evolve over lengthy periods of intimacy, but even so—
oh, I didn't know what to make of it.

She wouldn't be able to see me until after Christmas; she
urged me to get away for a few days, she thought I needed a
rest. I only had twenty-four hours off, I told her. But I did
have an uncle, my mother's brother, an old man who lived in
a small town on the south coast, and he'd written to me in
November inviting me to lunch on Christmas Day. At your

mother's prompting I now accepted the invitation, though
with some misgivings; I'd have preferred to indulge the emotions of my lover's heart in London, I'd have liked to fan the
flames of my unceasing obsessive desire to be with her sitting
alone over the gas fire in Jubilee Road. I see now how important it was that I go; for had I stayed in London I would
never have known Griffin Head, nor renewed acquaintance
with an uncle I hadn't seen since I was a boy.

Christmas in St. Basil's. The wash room up in theaters had
been decorated with bunting and streamers and everyone felt
festive. As we scrubbed for surgery there was energetic talk
about Germany, and the growing tensions between us. I realized, powdering my hands, the easier to draw off the rubber
gloves afterwards, that my attitude to the prospect of war had
changed, that I no longer felt the same grim fatalistic sense
of relish I used to feel, for now the future held promise for
me. Now I feared the upheaval and destruction that war would
bring—now I had something to lose. And so, I realized, had
the rest of the surgical staff, this was clear from their conversation. Cushing of course had the last word. "It all goes to
demonstrate," he said, when we'd gone through to theaters,
and were about to begin a complicated visceral sympathec-
tomy, "that the British, politically speaking, are split down
the middle." We stood with our forearms bent upward, hands
pointed to the ceiling, as the scrub nurse gowned us, tying
the bows behind our backs. "Rationally," said Cushing, "we
adhere to democratic principles. Emotionally, imagina-
tively"—hemostats clicked, sutures were snipped, the wound
was a forest of loop-handled steel instruments—"we indulge
a rich appetite for costume and ritual. Hence our adoration of
the monarchy. It's a damn sight more benign"—here he cut
the first of the small preganglionic fibers emanating from the
thoracic and lumbar cords—"than what the Germans do.
Where we have royalty"—now he frowned, barked out a few
terse orders, called for more retraction—"they have the Nazi

party." Then he began talking about diastolic blood pressure, and the arteriolar vasculature, and the operation went forward. Speak for yourself, I thought. It wasn't royalty I was worried about, it was your mother. If war came—as it probably would—and we lost it—as we probably would—what place would there be in that new world for love?

My uncle's name was Henry Bird and he lived in a small white villa overlooking the esplanade in Griffin Head. Oh, I need hardly describe the town to you! Often enough we've amused ourselves on the subject of Griffin Head—only through your eyes was I ever able to see the place with humor and affection, before you came I was bitterly unhappy here. It is an Edwardian sea resort, and in the years before the war its residents were elderly and invalid for the most part, retired to the coast after careers in the professions or the stock market or banking in London, or in the colonial or diplomatic service abroad. Peace and quiet is what the place offered them, and convalescence in comfort. A dozen or so hotels and boardinghouses catered to the small number of visitors who came during the summer, but there were few attractions for the more vulgar type of holidaymaker, hence the town's reputation for a particularly stagnant form of English gentility.

I went down on Christmas Eve. A frail but spirited man, my uncle Henry, he'd spent his life as a sort of glorified manservant to a wealthy member of the local aristocracy, since deceased, who'd apparently been generous in her will. Intensely sociable, charming and effusive, and marvelously elegant in a dark blue suit with a white shirt and a pink bow tie, he greeted me with great warmth—"Lovely to see you, dear boy!"—and made us each a powerful cocktail. Sitting in his small, neat drawing room I listened with half a mind as he talked happily about his antiques. My arrival had coincided with a wild winter storm: salt-drenched gales scoured the buildings along the front, and waves broke against the seawall with such force that columns of water were hurled thirty feet high then dashed to white spray and foam. I gazed out of Henry's bay window and felt a sort of correspondence of the elemental wildness outside with the turbulence in myself: this, I thought, rather savoring the conceit, is the weather of my heart. Pathetic fallacy I daresay, but no less powerful for that. Over game hen with mashed potatoes and brussels sprouts, and a nice little claret he'd been saving for the occasion, and a rich plum pudding, and nuts and dates and cheese and port, I listened to Henry as he lingered among his memories of the old days in the great houses. "Life is very different now of course," he murmured, mellow and maudlin with port. "So much has changed." He sighed. "Sometimes I lie in bed at night and listen to the waves turning far out to sea, and I think it's all a dream, only the sea is real."

After lunch we went for a walk. In our hats and overcoats we made our way down to the front, down through the old part of the town with its steep narrow cobblestoned streets that aroused in my imagination pictures of Griffin Head as it must have been in the 1700s, a smugglers' haven of peglegged old salts in cocked hats and earrings. The wind drove salty rain into our faces and flattened our clothes against our bodies and forced us to clutch our hats tightly to our heads. With some difficulty we managed to cross the esplanade and stand in the gale on the seawall, watching the waves exploding and crashing, one after another, then falling away, sucking and dragging at the loosened shingle piled against the battered wooden groins that sliced the beach into sections and streamed with seaweed. Henry's scarf I remember fluttered about him like an ensign. He grinned wildly at me and shouted remarks I couldn't hear.

After a few moments of this we turned our backs to the wind and pushed eastward along the empty seafront toward the pier, which was almost lost in a haze of spray and rain. Beneath dark, lowering clouds gulls rose and wheeled and

screamed in the wind. Henry wouldn't go out along the pier,
so I staggered out by myself and stood gripping the railing
behind the pavilion at the far end, as the violence thrashed
and gushed about me. My head was soaked and streaming
with salt spray, a wonderful sensation. I turned and gazed
inland, saw through the scrim of hazy rain the stormswept
little town clustered on its hill in tiers, the old part at the
bottom, the neat terraces of white Regency villas higher up,
and higher still the Gothic Revival mansions brooding behind
tall hedges and old trees. Despite the blurring of the weather
the effect was one of strong vertical accents, of sharp outlines
and jagged profiles, and I exulted in the rather odd, wild,
toothy beauty of it all, for it was, as I say, somehow expressive
of my own condition and feeling. Further to the east the cliffs
stood out against the angry sky, a few proud old houses on
the summit; one of them was Elgin, though of course I didn't
know this yet; beyond, the visible world was lost in the gloom
of approaching dusk.

After we got back to the house Henry told me, over tea
and hot crumpets, a curious story about the town. To the west
of Griffin Head, he said, there was once a church which stood
sixty feet back from the edge of a cliff. Over the years the
sea ate steadily into the cliff, until the destruction of the
church seemed imminent, and it was desanctified and abandoned. The stonework crumbled, the tower and south wall
collapsed, and ivy crawled thickly over what was left. Not
surprisingly an atmosphere of melancholy desolation grew up
around the place, and there were reports of unearthly forms
flitting among the ruins. Then one wild night in the winter
of 1925 a great storm tore out the cliff and took the remains
of the church with it, and the next morning the stones were
strewn all along the beach. What disturbed the local people
was not the loss of the church, that had been expected for
years; no, what disturbed them, said Henry (whose spirits had
been quite revived by our walk), was that the sea had bitten

into the graveyard, and in the face of the new cliff could quite clearly be made out the forms of human skeletons. They're still there, he said. "Come down and see me again, dear boy, and I'll show you the bones."

A melancholy aura pervades any institution at Christmastime. Despite the best efforts of the staff, asylum bonhomie only serves to point up what is lacking: all that is intimate, familial and domestic. When I came into St. Basil's late that night I encountered an atmosphere of gray gloom. The train journey back from the sea had already done much to destroy my exultation of the afternoon. My compartment was dirty and unheated, and I'd sat peering out into the darkness and smoking cigarette after cigarette, and trying not to shiver, for my overcoat was still damp despite Henry's gallant attempt to dry it in front of the fire. Only a few more days till I saw your mother again, but even that thought failed to ignite my imagination, so overwhelmingly antiromantic is the effect of traveling by rail in the south of England in winter. Sharing the compartment with me was a weary young woman with two children who had consumed far too much sugar earlier in the day and were now, predictably, suffering the consequences. We were all suffering the consequences. I was never so glad in my life to see Victoria Station. Back in Jubilee Road I huddled on top of the gas fire in my paisley dressing gown with a cup of hot tea laced with gin and felt sorry for myself.

The days between Christmas and the New Year have always seemed to me a sort of black hole in the calendar. Days of desolation. But about halfway through Boxing Day I found myself thinking of your mother's impending visit, and so near did it suddenly seem that I felt the familiar surge, the visceral tingle and warmth, and my spirits began to rise. There was a letter for me when I got home from St. Basil's on the twenty-ninth, in that by-now-familiar hand: would I meet her in the Two Eagles? I was disappointed that she wasn't coming to

Jubilee Road, but I understood why, the cold of course. Perhaps we would come back afterwards.

I was there early, and she was late—and the twenty or so minutes that I sat alone provided several intense jabs of panic, as I considered the possibility of her not appearing. But at last she arrived, rather flustered, rather distracted. "A large gin, darling," she said, "I need it."

"I thought you weren't coming," I said. "I thought something had happened to you."

"Really? What would have happened to me?" She was opening her cigarette case. Her eyes never left my face as she put the cigarette between her lips. I pulled my matches from my pocket, and as she leaned forward to the flame her eyes were still on mine. "Sorry," I said, "am I being silly?"

She inhaled deeply and shook her head. A pale hand fluttered across the table and settled on my sleeve for a moment. "You're not being silly," she said with seriousness. "Thank you for worrying."

"I'll get your gin."

When I sat down again she said, "I have a present for you."

"I have one for you too," I said. "You look tired, has it been difficult?"

"I'm not sleeping well," she said as she groped in her handbag. "I don't know why."

"Things awkward at home?" For a moment I glimpsed in my mind's eye the face of the senior pathologist, and heard his ringing baritone—"It's the *pathos* that conditions the *logos*, doctor!"—and then McGuinness's acid tones—"There's something primitive makes a man go into pathology—*I pity the wife.*" She brought out a small object wrapped in green tissue paper. "I don't imagine you'll like it," she said, "I just thought of you when I saw it, so I bought it. It was an impulse."

"An impulse," I said, as I took it from her. She hadn't answered my question about things at home, but great tenderness was aroused at the idea of her thinking of me on seeing something in a shop window. That I should be present in her mind when we were not together, as she was in mine—to be told this, actually to hear it from her lips rather than simply wondering if her response to me mirrored mine to her—it affected me more strongly than I'd imagined possible. We had said so pitifully little about our feelings! Yet all the time, in the obscure depths of the heart, something had been growing: love. The growth of love. I unfolded the tissue paper and discovered wrapped within it a piece of glass shaped like a pebble, flat on the bottom, with a fly inside it. "Good God," I said, "now how did they get it in there?" I held it up to the light. Whole and perfect, a common housefly, *Musca domestica*, was suspended in the glass as though frozen in flight, as though the air through which it moved had solidified abruptly about it, trapping it to eternity. As I turned it in my fingers daggers of light flashed and splintered from the smooth curved surface. "Isn't it curious?" she said. "Do you like it? I thought it might make a paperweight. Or you could clench it in your fist in moments of fury."

"I'll keep it in my pocket," I said. I put it back on the table, in its crumply nest of tissue paper. "It will bring me luck."

"Of some description."

I stepped round the table and stooped to kiss her lips. She turned away slightly and gave me her cheek. Her hand came up and touched the side of my face. The kiss lasted a second or two; then came a brief flurry of confusion, me losing control, kissing her neck, then abruptly sitting down and pushing my hand through my hair while she, with a small smile, watched me. "I know," she said. "It's difficult. I'm sorry, darling." I shook my head and lifted my drink slightly, to her.

When it came time to leave she still hadn't answered my question about things at home. I rose from the table and slipped the fly-in-glass into my trouser pocket, where through the material I could feel it hard against my thigh.

Later that evening I was in my room getting ready to go to

St. Basil's. I was changing my shirt in front of the mirror in the door of my wardrobe, the fly-in-glass on the table behind me with the desk lamp shining directly upon it. When I'd briefly lost control in the Two Eagles, and kissed her neck, she'd said, "I'm sorry. It's difficult, I know." But what had she meant—*what* was difficult? Sustaining our passion under clandestine conditions? Or something else—not going back to Jubilee Road to make love, perhaps?

Then a little later she'd suddenly felt sure she could hear Ratcliff in the next bar. I'd listened, and heard him too; he was talking about the role of the pancreatic hormone in glucide metabolism. We'd stared at each other, aghast, for several moments—I went up to the counter and cautiously peered round into the next bar—to find a group of commercial travelers telling each other jokes. This of course was symptomatic of the deeply furtive nature of our relationship, and it troubled me. Never had I imagined that when I met the woman I was destined to love she would be married to another man—not just another man, but another doctor, a colleague. Oh, but Ratcliff Vaughan was an odd, cold creature, I told myself, barely human, a *pathologist,* for the love of God! Whatever went on in Plantagenet Gardens, it hardly bore thinking about, this sad, lovely woman and that primitive. With these thoughts running in my head I attempted again to tie my tie; my fingers were shaking and I couldn't seem to get the bloody thing right, and I hate more than anything an ill-tied tie.

The tie was tied, but still I didn't move away from the wardrobe mirror. Oh God. Possibly my whole thinking was wrong. Do you know the feeling—you may not be old enough—the ghastly lurch of shock, I mean, that comes when, having thought about a thing for days on end, and then suddenly encountering a point of view in which previously unimaginable categories are employed, all values abruptly shift—?

Ten minutes later I left the house and made my way up

Jubilee Road (it was a cold, windy night) toward St. Basil's. I was on Accident and Casualty, but my shift was happily uneventful. Around two o'clock I admitted a man whose hand had been horribly crushed under heavy machinery during night work in a factory. I called McGuinness in, for the damage was extensive. As I applied Vaseline dressings to the wound I thought about the commercial travelers in the Two Eagles; suddenly—it hurts me to remember this—suddenly the affair with your mother, viewed against the reality of a man in pain and in danger of losing his hand, seemed so foolish and indulgent that I felt myself ridiculous. But it *mattered*, this I could not deny, *she* mattered, I loved her and *love* mattered— how then could it be ridiculous? Yet it was. I felt the hard lump of the fly-in-glass in my pocket. Love is what we crave, but it vanishes like a dream on exposure to a certain sort of reality, such were my thoughts in the few moments it took me to apply a pad of Vaseline gauze steeped in bactericide to the bloody mangle of flesh and bone.

Then McGuinness appeared; examined the damage; turned to me and shook his head. We took the man up to theaters. The procedure is straightforward: you have to leave a flap of skin so there's something to sew back over the stump, then with a heavy amputating knife you saw off the mess below the level of the flap, toss it all into a pail (whose contents later go down to the incinerator room in the basement) and stitch up what's left. It was the first time I'd cut a man's hand off, and it made me shiver. We were clever though. We saved his apposition. He would still be able to hold things with his thumb and forefinger, the only digits he had left on that hand.

When I left St. Basil's the next morning I was tired, but clear once more in both my heart and my conscience, for a sustained bout of surgical activity had dissipated the anxiety that the meeting in the Two Eagles had aroused. Now here's an odd thing. Did you know (though how would you?) that in some doctors, surgical work has an aphrodisiac effect? I find this hard to understand. Amputation, especially, fills me with distaste for all bodily functions, and when I came away from the wards my desire was generally for nothing more physical than a volume of poetry and a glass of gin. So it was that morning. I got back to Jubilee Road, changed into my pajamas and dressing gown, and after a few minutes with Keats slipped into deep dreamless sleep. I was awoken in the late afternoon by a knock on the door. It was Desmond Kelly, with a letter from your mother. Delicately scented, in that neat spidery hand of hers, it said she was sorry for being such a bore yesterday evening, would I forgive her? She loved me and would see me again very soon.

Soon we were meeting at every opportunity. It wasn't easy for either of us; your mother hated telling lies, while for me, getting away from St. Basil's for even an hour required that another doctor cover for me, usually McGuinness, and though I invented a story about an elderly relative who was desperately ill he soon became skeptical, and a joke grew up around "Dr. Haggard's sick auntie." In fact it was Henry I had in mind.

But though it might involve just twenty minutes in the Two Eagles, or a teashop, each meeting served to sustain the taut string of feeling that bound us together. We would sit at the very back of the teashop and hold hands over the hot-buttered teacakes, and murmur our small talk, our lovers' talk, while under the table our knees touched, and your mother would slip off a shoe and rub a small silken foot against my calf, which instantly aroused me. Encounters like this served only to inflame my impatience to be alone with her again. Naturally I never went to Plantagenet Gardens, she always came to Jubilee Road. I've told you about that room, it was a large, untidy, high-ceilinged room with a few big pieces of dark battered furniture. There were books and papers in piles on the floor, and a skull for an ashtray. On the wall, among my landscapes and sunsets, hung an elegant framed Vesalius print my father gave me shortly before he died.

That scholar's room now began to change. It began to reflect your mother. The harsh glare of the overhead bulb gave way, with the arrival of a pair of pale blue ceramic lamps, to a low soft shadowy glow. She brought a beautiful Persian rug on which we lay together in front of the gas fire. She hung a length of fabric across the bedroom door, replaced the sheets and installed candles. Pots and bottles of unguents apeared, creams and lotions and perfumes. My quarters were gradually feminized. My cell became a boudoir.

This then was our private sanctuary; our intimacy, our love, our passion, all found expression here. Your mother was at times voracious, feline, avid for me; at other times slow, voluptuous and careless; she was a woman of many moods. I remember her nested in the pillows and linen of my big bed in a superb state of languor, her elegant clothing in immodest disarray, a pale lovely creature suffused with the glow of profound physical pleasure. I remember too how sometimes we'd be together in the Two Eagles and such would be the impatience generated by her urgent sexual need of me that we would hurry back to Jubilee Road even if only for eight or ten minutes, and barely get the door shut behind us before we were on the floor and pulling off her silvery silk underpants. Afterwards I'd lie back and smoke and stare at the ceiling and feel a sort of swimmy, dissolving sensation sweep over me like mist. I'd weep a little and then laugh in an abashed sort of way as your mother, heavy-lidded and indolent, lay in my arms and gave me little kisses and murmured endearments, darling, sweetheart, precious Edward. She told me how deeply it excited her when I became excited, how this being so fiercely desired aroused desire in her, and how my silence, and my intentness, made me seem a stranger to her, and how it alarmed her but fascinated her that my sexual character differed so dramatically from my social self.

She had never (she said) felt herself the object of such passion before.

A brief period, then, of almost unblemished bliss. What blemishes there were were the blemishes all lovers know. Everything was so fraught! I remember once we argued about Hitler. "So alarmist," she remarked, glancing at a man's newspaper as we left the Two Eagles after a swift drink one evening, "all this talk of war with Germany. Hitler doesn't want war."

"Not this year, certainly," I said. We were standing on the pavement looking for a taxi.

"Not any year," she said. "I think he's created order and stability in the country. He won't risk that."

"But the man's a monster!" I cried. "He's a megalomaniac! A murderer!"

"He's an authoritarian," she said, "and that's alien to this political culture, but they do things differently in Germany."

"They most certainly do."

"Their history hasn't given them the experience of democracy that ours has."

"Darling, it's not about history!"

"Can anything be said to be not about history?"

"Yes. Fascism."

I suppose the same argument occurred over thousands of dinner tables every night, in the months before Munich, before Prague. But for us to argue, even about politics—it left me feeling utterly desolate, as though I'd lost her. I was miserable until I saw her again. She dismissed it with an airy wave. "Oh darling," she said, "we were just talking about Hitler. What a sensitive soul you are—you mustn't take it so seriously."

But I did. My life now contained only two types of time, time with her and time without her; one paradise, the other hell. There were the small agonies: waiting for her, and becoming panicked if she was late. This was torment. I would try and explain her absence to myself until at last it became impossible not to assume that disaster had occurred and she was lost to me forever. Then she would appear, and find me affecting pathos, trying to hide my joy at seeing her, and so wasting whole, precious minutes of the few fleeting hours we were to be allowed. There was my tendency, too, after each meeting, to dissect and analyze every word and gesture she'd made, examining each in trembling apprehension that it signified on her part impatience, or boredom, and therefore imminent rejection. There were even moments (the man with the mangled hand was one) when I *doubted* when the whole fragile tissue of feeling became somehow unreal and I could not hold on to it, though the doubt vanished the instant I saw her.

But we grew careless. Caught up in love's dream, feeling invulnerable, and touched with grace, we grew careless. Perhaps it was inevitable. Perhaps we needed, unconsciously, to precipitate a crisis—perhaps we *had to!* I don't know. I don't know what made her come to the hospital that night. She was at times subject to black moods, to brief attacks of melancholy, and I've come to believe that Ratcliff provoked this unhappiness in her, that he was the source of her pain, and that she came to me for solace. I did what I could, believe me, I felt for her, and it was torture for me to see her suffer, as it's torture to see *you* suffer, precious boy—! But I was on the ward one night when a porter appeared and told me that a Mrs. Piker-Smith was waiting to see me downstairs.

I hurried down to the lobby; it was your mother of course. She was in the black fur, and a close-fitting black hat with a net veil spangled with tiny black stars. "I shouldn't really leave the ward," I whispered. She lifted a gloved hand and laid a finger against my lips.

The lobby of St. Basil's is an echoing, pillared hall with marbled floors and portraits of governors past and present hung on the walls. By day it is like a railway station, milling with people, a din of noise; by night it is silent, and thick with shadows; deserted but for a cleaner with her bucket and mop. From the back of the hall a stone staircase descends by two flights to Pathology, Medical Records, and the incinerator room. Beside the staircase, against the back wall, and hidden from view by a pillar, stands a wooden bench, and I followed your mother, tiny veiled figure in a huge black fur, heels clicking on the tiles, across the lobby and behind the pillar to this bench. We sat down. She turned to me, lifting the veil and folding it carefully back upon her hat. Her face was in shadow, for little light penetrated the space behind the pillar. Her lipstick looked black in the gloom. I tried to take her in my arms but she pulled away, turned her back to me and groped for cigarettes. I lit two, gave her one, and we smoked; all evening, she said, she'd been restless and on edge. Her voice had a sort of somber, breathless urgency to it. Ratcliff had gone to some function at the Royal Society of Medicine, leaving her alone in the house, and eventually she'd been unable to read any longer and had gone up to her room, intending to put on her coat and go for a walk. It was then that the idea of visiting me at St. Basil's had come to her.

After a first recoil of shock at the audacity of it, and the risk involved, it had occurred to her to wear her veil. Entering the hospital and waiting for me in the lobby had aroused anxiety, but now, she said, she felt calm. She leaned toward me, threw away her cigarette, and this time allowed me to kiss her. The pervasive hospital smell, bleach and antiseptic, mingled in my nostrils with her perfume. I took her gloved hands and in a low voice told her I wanted to spend all night with her. She seized my face and kissed me several times, small, rapid kisses, murmuring no, telling me that I must get back to work and she must go home. I lost control at that point, and so did she, and kissing, now, with passionate urgency, we fumbled at each other's clothing, pulling at buttons and clips, and we managed, somehow, to get my trousers open, and her skirt pushed up, and still in the big fur coat she climbed into my lap and there on the bench at the back of the lobby of one of the great London teaching hospitals we made hasty passionate love that left us dazed and panting and clinging to one another in disordered lethargy and I (as usual) began to cry, which aroused your mother to the realities of the situation, so stroking my head and making little tender clucking noises she gently pushed me away and readjusted her clothing and by the flame of her cigarette lighter attended to her face in the mirror of her powder compact. My own excitement subsided. I buttoned my trousers and retrieved my stethoscope from under the bench. I became aware of how peaceful the lobby was, the stillness and silence curiously restful, as though we were in a cathedral. I turned back to her. The flame of her lighter trembled as a small draft crept among the pillars, and the obscure, flickering reflection of her face was for an instant eerily distorted in the tiny glass of the compact. Satisifed, finally, that no trace of the recent brief passion remained, she snapped it shut. "Now back to work," she whispered, and we rose to our feet. After a last embrace I made off through the shadows.

Suddenly, footsteps! From the staircase appeared Miggs with a rack of test tubes, and I saw your mother turn toward him. "Evening, Mrs. Vaughan," he said, without apparent surprise, and passed on. Good God, her veil! She'd forgotten about it! She hadn't replaced her veil!

Later she told me about the journey back to Plantagenet Gardens. Miggs had seen her—this thought was of course uppermost in her mind, but the odd thing was, instead of feeling acute alarm she felt exhilarated—why? Because she was adrift in love's dream, and nothing could touch her because nothing else mattered—was this it? Or was there some other reason, some perverse longing for crisis, or the ecstasy of the abyss—James, I *don't know!*

•   •   •

Perhaps you do. Perhaps you understand her better than I do.
We didn't ever solve the problem of how to talk to each other
about her, did we? After the evening you asked me if she'd
"thrown herself" at me I realized it was impossible—that is,
that the son of a beautiful mother could share with that woman's lover any sort of common language with regard to her, or
not, at least, in any *direct* way. I couldn't speak to you about
the sexual expression of our love. I could never tell you what
happened to me just by *looking* at her—watching her walk
into a room in front of me, a tearoom, the saloon bar of the
Two Eagles, even watching her cross to the window in Jubilee
Road—she was so straight and slim and lovely I yearned for
her with every cell of my body. She'd turn and she'd see it
in my eyes, and seeing it, she would feel the desire aroused
in *her,* and then we would be in each other's arms. I loved
her as a woman, her skin, her small perfect limbs, her lips,
her hair. She loved me as a man, she adored this ill-propor-
tioned body of mine, she adored my penis, adored its en-
gorgement,   thick-veined   and   large-headed—not   unlike
myself!—her fingers were skillful with my trouser buttons,
and the mere touch of them upon the fabric quickened my
arousal such that by the time she pulled me free of my clothing
I would be as eager for her small soft tender mouth, her little
teeth, as she was for me, and this lasted only long enough to
become so intolerably exquisite that nothing would do but
that I be inside her, and this she would effect with those quick
deft fingers and then we'd cling together and be one until
orgasm swept us onto another, higher plane—small wonder
afterwards that I cried! None of this I could ever tell you,
though I wanted to, for it was the direct erotic manifestation
of our spiritual communion.

As, in a way, are you.

I remember it was Mrs. Gregor who first set me thinking,
after you'd been to tea one afternoon. She'd brought us up a

tray and on it a plate of macaroons and a Dundee cake. I've a sweet tooth myself and will often work all day on a piece of chocolate, so I didn't notice that between us we ate all the macaroons *and* the Dundee cake—but Mrs. Gregor did, she was fond of you. "That young man likes his cake," she remarked, when I came back in from seeing you off and found her in the hall putting on her coat in front of the mirror. I was about to go into the surgery. "Oh?" I said, and I don't know why this is—call it a doctor's intuition—but I paused there and paid close attention to what she was telling me. Some sort of warning bell went off, I suppose. Mrs. Gregor was straightening her hat. Without taking her eyes off her reflection in the mirror she said: "I'd thought that cake would do us another week."

"Did we eat it all, Mrs. Gregor?"

"I don't know that you did much of the eating, doctor. You've never been much of a one for Dundee cake."

I went into the surgery and closed the door behind me. So. One more thing I knew about you. You resembled your mother, you blushed easily, you flew Spitfires—and you loved sweet things. I think at some level of my unconscious mind I began to form a hazy, tentative hypothesis. I stress unconscious, it was weeks before I had a clear clinical picture. But I think even in the first days of our friendship I was alert to the symptoms that would eventually organize themselves into a diagnostic pattern, a dramatically disturbing pattern, not only for you but for me, too, as your friend and physician.

Yes, perhaps I should have spotted it sooner. Oh, but it was a cold, cold winter, this last one, the coldest in forty-five years and never have I had such grief from Spike since the early days—my God he was vicious! I understand why, of course—damaged bone grinding against its seating in the pelvis—but that does little to help. Nor was it just late at night, as is generally the case, this winter Spike was active all day, and all night too. I was forced to rely rather more extensively than usual on the morphia; I needed a shot just to get through morning surgery, and another after lunch for afternoon rounds, if I was to be any use to my patients at all (what patients I still had). So it was not an easy winter, and the effects of it lasted through the spring and into the summer. Which makes me wonder if I shouldn't have realized sooner that something was seriously wrong.

Daffodils were coming up in the parks of London—Nazis were marching triumphantly into Vienna—and for your mother and me the first augurs of disaster made themselves known. It can't have gone unnoticed that I was less single-mindedly focused on my work than I'd once been, and it wasn't just the hours here and there when I slipped away for trysts with your mother while McGuinness covered for me. All doctors make these arrangements, if they're to have any private life at all. No, it was more a matter of attitude. My heart wasn't in it anymore, and this sad fact was demonstrated to the entire hospital with the ghastly mess I made one morning of a simple appendicectomy.

It's a delicate thing, opening a man's belly. You draw the knife across the skin, the flesh parts, you clamp the severed vessels, sponge the blood, suture and tie, cut through the yellow fat beneath, then the fascia, clamp, sponge, suture, tie, then the peritoneum, and so on. But I went in with such force I cut right through the fascia with the first stroke of the knife, opening numerous blood vessels, and then, while tying them off, somehow sewed the end of my rubber glove into the wound. I was rather shaken by this, and botched the rest of the operation. The patient recovered, eventually, but he had a complicated convalescence and became enormously distended, with the result that the nursing staff referred to him as "Dr. Haggard's pregnant man." What particularly irritated Vincent Cushing was that the rubber glove story went all over St. Basil's, and as I was part of his team he was subjected indirectly to ridicule. This rankled.

He called me into his office. He stood gazing out of his

window onto the courtyard below, his pudgy little hands clasped behind his back. "Dr. Haggard," he said at last, "you've been on my service for six months."

"Yes sir."

He turned. He frowned. Then: "Surgery is the most exacting branch of medicine."

Another pause. He went to his desk and sat down. I was anticipating more of the same, but instead he looked up at me and said, "I can get you transferred to the medical service tomorrow, and you would go with a strong letter of referral." Good God, was I being *sacked?* This was a shock. "Is that what you want, doctor?"

"Actually no, sir," I said, "not at all. I would like to finish my residency with you."

"I see." Pause, cough, frown. "Why, then, doctor, have you apparently lost your taste for the work? You know what's required of you."

"Yes, I do." I pushed a hand through my hair. "I've been preoccupied. I know I shouldn't let it interfere but I'm afraid it has. It won't happen again."

"Preoccupied—?"

"Family problems."

"Oh?"

"My uncle has been ill."

"Something serious, I take it."

"Cancer. Inoperable."

"I'm sorry. You're close to him?"

"My people are dead, sir. He's my only relative."

He was a hard but not a heartless man, he said, and he maintained high standards on his service because it was his responsibility to train able surgeons—though I hadn't forgotten the business with Eddie Bell. "I do sympathize," he said. "At the same time, as I'm sure I need not remind you, the physician has not the luxury of dwelling on his personal problems while he is attending patients."

"I know."

"You may make a surgeon, Dr. Haggard, I don't rule out the possibility. Frankly I'm unhappy with your performance. I shall be watching your work closely in future."

That was all. I was not a happy man as I walked away from Cushing's office. I seemed on the point of throwing away a career in surgery for love of your mother. This must not happen, I told myself, though the truth was, in my heart I didn't care. I didn't care. All professional ambition had paled and withered in the shadow of this grand passion, and I'd have happily exchanged a lifetime of surgical work for twenty-four uninterrupted hours alone with her.

I did try, in the days following, to do better, but it wasn't easy. My mind wandered constantly. Faced with a suppurating abscess, I saw the smooth white skin of your mother's breast. Removing a dirty dressing, and finding a black patch of necrotic tissue, I imagined placing delicate kisses on her belly. Encountering death, I remembered her clinging to me and gasping with pleasure on a bench at the back of the hospital lobby. Wherever my eye fell, wherever I saw disease, or injury, or death, I also found hints and glimpses of beauty, and the difficulty lay in keeping my attention on morbidity when all my soul cried out to love.

But what place was there in this world for love?

I learned later that Ratcliff had found out almost immediately about your mother being in the hospital that night, but waited some days before asking for an explanation. Why did he wait? From what she told me I had the impression that he must have been frightened of the truth, of discovering just how dissatisfied she was with the marriage, in other words how badly he had failed her. But then, as the days passed, and she still did not allude to it, he must have worried at it with growing irritation. It was either of no importance, I imagined him thinking—which was unlikely—or else she was concealing it from him. But if she was concealing it, she must have known that Miggs would talk, in which case she would surely have brought it up, in order to allay any doubt or suspicion on his part, and this she had not done.

April came, the sky was pale as pearls, and the trees along Plantagenet Gardens were hazy with buds. It was on a warm evening in April, your mother told me, that Ratcliff first attempted to face the rift that had for years been opening between them, and which in recent months had widened at such an alarming rate. The dining room was a somber room, not a room that invited intimacy, and your mother had always disliked it, though recently, she said, she'd often thought of *me* there, and this, she said, had changed its associations, had superimposed upon the shapeless mass of memories of desultory meals with Ratcliff the idea of *love*, where it shimmered like a mist over a swamp: at this table, and upon this chair, she had sat thinking of her lover, and now the furniture glowed.

Ratcliff of course knew nothing of this. "Have you," he began, "thought any more about Scotland this summer?"

The last time he'd brought up the subject your mother had felt distinctly irritated at the idea of leaving London, and said something vague and noncommittal. "Scotland," she murmured now, setting down her knife and fork and touching her lips with her napkin; Iris had served them a nice shoulder of lamb. "No, I haven't. We should discuss it when James is here, I suppose."

"Oh, I doubt we'll see much of him this summer. I've told him he can start flying lessons."

"You haven't! Oh Ratcliff."

This was a shock. To think of you flying aeroplanes—you were still (in her mind) a child. She said this to Ratcliff. "No he's not," he said. "He's not a child anymore. We have to accept this."

"But it's so dangerous!"

"He has to try it. If he can't fly with our blessing, he'll fly without it."

And then a curious thing happened. All her resistance to

the idea, the surge of maternal anxiety it had provoked—it all just evaporated, leaving her strangely indifferent. Let him fly, then, she thought. If he wants to fly—if Ratcliff wants him to fly—so be it. She gave a small shrug of her shoulders. "Very well," she murmured, reaching for the mint sauce. Ratcliff frowned at her as he tore a bread roll part. What did this mean, this sudden lapse into unconcern? (She was in love, of course, that's what it meant, and like me could think of little else.) "Then you don't object?" he said.

"What does it matter if I object or not? You seem to have decided the issue."

"Frances, what *is* the matter with you these days?" A note of exasperation here. "You seem to care about nothing any-more. Don't you owe me the courtesy of an explanation?"

She raised her eyebrows at this. "Frankly I don't think I do." She gazed at him across the table and after a moment he took off his spectacles and rubbed his eyes with his thumb and index finger. She caught a faint whiff of formalin. How pregnant must have been the few seconds of silence that followed that candid gaze! What a complex private history underscored that silence, the long years of emotional nego-tiation they had endured to reach this present state of mutual balanced toleration! The membrane of marital order could take so much stress and no more, to this they had both been sensitive for some time, neither of them willing to see it torn. But something had changed, this much was clear, and Ratcliff persevered. "Something has happened," he said. "I don't know what it is, and I'm not altogether sure I want to. But you do owe me this, you know, you owe me at the least a modicum of candor."

Again she lifted her eyebrows and said nothing. Her silence seemed to infuriate him. "Well? What do you say to that? What's your answer?"

"What's your question?" she retorted. She felt suddenly terribly weary, she told me afterwards. It was all so tedious, so predictable.

Ratcliff sighed. He poured himself more wine. Iris came in to clear away the dinner plates. They generally went straight from the main course to cheese and fruit and coffee, if they had no guests. When Iris had left the room Ratcliff said flatly, "What were you doing in the hospital the night I was at the RSM?"

"Was I?" she said. "Could I have the grapes, please, Ratcliff?"

"You met Miggs. He told me, of course. He thought it odd that you should be there at that time of the evening. So do I."

"For God's sake!" She was certainly not going to be cross-examined like some errant medical student! "How dare you speak to me like that! How dare you sit there and tell me that you and Miggs find my behavior odd! What else does Miggs say about me?"

"I don't discuss you with Miggs. As well you know. I merely ask: what were you doing in the hospital?"

"And I tell you, I resent bitterly—*bitterly*—the implication that I was 'doing' anything that would oblige me to give you an explanation."

"Nevertheless I ask you for an explanation."

"And on principle I refuse to give you one."

They were both bolt upright in their chairs, she told me, tense and furious. And what happened then, I wanted to know? Your mother gave a slight shrug. He backed off, she said. But why, I cried? It seemed most peculiar. I expect he doesn't really want to know, she said. She described how he sank back against his chair. "All right," he said, tight-lipped now, controlling his anger. He folded his napkin precisely, rolled it tight and thrust it into its ring. "We'll talk about it later."

"I'm going upstairs," your mother said coldly. "Please ask Iris to bring up my coffee."

"Frances."

She paused at the door.

"I apologize for losing my temper."

She went out without another word. She hadn't heard the last of it. Oh, it was becoming much too complicated, she wished it were all simple again. Damn him! Damn him for smelling a rat!

"Oh damn Ratcliff. What a bloody nuisance. Were you very upset, my darling?" It was eleven o'clock in the morning of a fine day in the middle of April, and your mother and I were in my flat in Jubilee Road. She'd been undecided whether she should tell me about it, and had said nothing immediately; but I'd quickly realized that all was not well, and after some concerned probing she'd told me everything, or almost everything; actually I'd begun to suspect that she never gave me a full account of what went on between herself and Ratcliff, perhaps because she could not convey the deep and subtle pattern in the fabric of that long, complicated relationship, its contradictory figures of attachment, resentment, and neglect. It made me feel desperate, being excluded from the hermetic web of her marriage. What I never really grasped was the idea that love may languish, even die, while attachment endures. By this stage I fervently desired her to leave Ratcliff and live with me, at whatever cost; but though I may have hinted to her of this I had never put it to her in frank and unambiguous terms.

There were flowers on the table, a large bunch of tiger lilies that she had brought. She had introduced flowers into my flat early in the relationship. They were leafy-stemmed, bulbous lilies, the speckled, pale orange petals folded back to allow the trembling stigma to thrust forth stiffly amid its cluster of slender, anther-tipped filaments, and a strong shaft of morning sunshine had unerringly sought them out where they fountained in profusion from a simple white porcelain vase, also introduced into the flat by your mother.

"Was I upset? Yes, I was very upset. He made me feel like a criminal."

"I wish—"

"Yes?"

"Nothing." She was sitting in an armchair and I was on the Persian rug with my back against her legs, gazing at the ceiling. Our fingers were interlaced, probing and playing with one another. "Do you think of leaving him?"

It was asked tentatively. "Oh darling," she murmured, "what would I do?"

"Live with me?"

She said nothing, though our fingers continued to speak. Each of us sensed what would be involved in pursuing this line of thought. I was nervous, and classified it as faintheartedness, and despised myself for it. I knew that the conversation must be had soon, and when that happened I would take my courage in both hands and properly propose the very thing that now gave me such anxiety even to think about. "What's to be done?" I said quietly.

"I don't want to think about him," your mother said, and slipped out of the armchair and knelt on the rug beside me. "Lie down," she said, so I stretched out on the carpet with my hands clasped behind my head. I was in a sleeveless V-necked argyll jersey and gray flannels; she was in an elegant pale green tweed suit with boxy shoulders and a snug felt hat. She unbuttoned my trousers. Easing her skirt up over her thighs she carefully settled herself athwart me. She gazed down at me through half-closed eyes, and the smile on her lips was the one I remembered from that funeral. Her fingers were busy with the clips of her suspender belt. I rubbed the head of my penis against the soft skin of her inner thigh, above the top of her stocking. "What do you think you're doing?" she murmured. "Now don't get me all messed up, I'm having lunch with someone."

"I'm giving you a physical."

"Oh you are, are you." She lifted herself slightly and made some adjustment to her underwear such that I was able to slip just the crown inside her. "That's all you're allowed," she said, "it's more than you deserve."

I pushed up slightly—a small intake of breath. "Stop that," she whispered. Her eyes were closed, her chin lifted, her lips parted. "I'll be late."

Another small push: exquisitely tantalizing! "Who are you having lunch with?" The gas fire hissed in my ear.

"Mind your own business." Still with her eyes closed she suddenly sank down on me with a long soft groan. A tide of warmth swept through my body. "I'll have you struck off for this," she breathed. Ominous words.

As you lie here in my arms, as these memories sweep by, as the story unfolds, movement by movement, opening in my mind like a complex flower—I am filled with foreboding. For as with the clouds of war, so were the clouds of ending, of parting, of sorrow drawing close. "Love is a growing, or full constant light"—this I had experienced, and it had filled my heart with glory—"And his first minute, after noon, is night." That night now approached.

Betrayal. I am not exempt, none of us is. I betrayed Henry Bird, and the first inkling I had of it came the day after your mother and I made love on the floor of Jubilee Road. It came from Peter Martin. That morning a milkman had found yesterday's bottle still standing on Henry's doorstep. He'd raised the alarm, a policeman had broken in through the back door and discovered the old man unconscious on the kitchen floor. He was admitted to the cottage hospital and had not yet regained consciousness. "I am his physician," said Dr. Martin, "and he is not taking any medicine that I am aware of, so I think we may discount an overdose. I don't have to tell you," he went on, "that it's probably a stroke." I thanked him and hung up. The news shook me badly. It was not that Henry should have had a stroke (at his age cerebrovascular disease was common), it was, rather, the fact that I had been telling people he was seriously ill, so as to pursue my love affair. It was pure coincidence of course, so I told myself, but I couldn't escape the irrational conviction that this was my doing—that by imputing disease to the old man I had actually brought it on—*I* had made him ill.

Peter Martin telephoned me the next day. "I think," he said, "we can safely say he's had a massive cerebrovascular accident. What would you like me to do, doctor?"

I could picture it all too clearly, Henry lying in bed in the cottage hospital, his skin white as china, his hair fine as silk, looking as though he were fast asleep and dreaming of great houses. For a moment a wave of guilty sorrow almost overwhelmed me. Peter Martin broke the silence. "He seems," he said, "a little wheezy. I think perhaps we're seeing the early signs of pneumonia."

I understood what I was being asked. Pneumonia—the old man's friend. "I wouldn't advise giving him sulfonamides," I said.

"No, there's no point. You'll be coming down, then?"

"Yes."

"Then I look forward to meeting you. My house is Elgin, it's up on the cliffs."

There was nothing more to say. Henry was to be allowed to die in peace, and I would see to the funeral arrangements. I hung up the telephone feeling very bad indeed. A week later the pneumonia carried him off, but I didn't go down to Griffin Head to make the arrangements, nor did I attend the funeral. I was in traction.

It was a wet, windy night and the pub was almost empty. A girl stood behind the bar drying glasses and gazing across the room in an abstracted, unfocused manner. She was miles away.

The few lamps hanging from the ceiling in dusty globes emitted a gloomy, yellowish light redolent somehow of weariness and loss. A woman with Parkinson's sat at a table by the fire with a glass of stout, which she lifted to her lips with the trembling fingers of both hands. The clock behind the bar ticked mournfully; no one spoke. I was exhausted, having been on call for seventy-two hours, and your mother was in very low spirits indeed. I was much in need of sleep—failing that, of conviviality, stimulation—but none was forthcoming, and with what little energy I could muster I made an effort to cheer her. I set my elbows on the table and leaning forward took her hands. Her eyes briefly registered irritation, then softened slightly. Something in her sad face strained toward me but failed to emerge or connect. I had never seen her like this. "Tired?" I said.

She pulled her hands free and shook her head. "No. Oh I don't know, it's all such a bore."

"What's the matter?" It was not easy for either of us, with Ratcliff so suspicious. She touched her hair, looking not at me but off to one side, unable to meet my eye. "I start to wonder if it's worth the trouble," she said, "I can't"—she paused, and produced a sort of sigh, as though it was an effort just to voice the words—"I can't endure much more of this." Still without looking at me she groped for my hands. "What about me?" I whispered. Was it the end? A flurry of rain suddenly lashed the window and she startled nervously. After a while she began to speak calmly. "I don't have the strength for it, darling. He knows how to wear me down, and he'll do it, he'll drive you away no matter what you do. No matter how much you try to hold on to me he'll drive you away. He doesn't know who you are but he knows that you exist, and he won't tolerate it. He's too strong for me."

"Then leave him!"

"Oh darling." She lit a cigarette. There was impatience and scorn in her voice. "Leave him for what? To live on a registrar's

salary? Love in a hut. Not even that. You couldn't continue
at St. Basil's if you lived with me. Use your imagination."
   I was silent, reeling.
   "You don't even light my cigarettes anymore. It can't go
on, you must see that."
   "No!" A cry of pain, this. She turned to me and her eyes
briefly filled with tears. "I'm sorry, my darling, but we must
be sensible. There's James to think of too."
   After that there was no getting through to her. She didn't
have much time. We spent another ten minutes in that dreary
pub and a grim ten minutes it was. No sort of intimacy seemed
possible. I tried to arouse in her the familiar bonds of affection—complicity—recognition even—I just wanted her to
recognize me, give me back a glimmer of something real—
but it was as though her real self had sunk like a guttering
flame and all there was in its place was this ghastly brittle talk
of being sensible, and that deadness in her eyes and voice as
though the words she was speaking were detached from all
meaning and emotion. Never had she shown this face to me
before. Not only was she showing me the face, she was using
it as a screen for an emptiness, out of which issued nothing
but this lucid unfeeling talk of ending it. Only once did she
show any emotion, connect with me at all, and that was when
she pleaded with me not to try and make her change her
mind. It would only make things worse for her. Anyway, I'd
be better off without her, she said. I'd be well rid of her, she
said, she'd only cause me pain—and she made me promise.
There in the shabby little saloon bar of the Two Eagles, as
an old clock ticked and a lonely old woman with shaking hands
sat mumbling to herself in the corner, I gave in and promised
her I wouldn't try and make her change her mind. Why did
I do it? Because at that moment, worried, exhausted, and
depressed as I was, I saw no way out. So I promised. I only
broke that promise once, but oh, with what disastrous
consequences!

Now things began to move rather quickly. The following afternoon your father performed a postmortem on a body pulled out of the Thames just below Lambeth Bridge. It had been in the river for at least two months, and the stench of it quickly spread through the entire hospital. It took him little more than an hour, by which time he had the entire heart and slices of all the other organs laid out on a tray that went into the refrigerator, covered with a damp cloth, for gross examination in the morning. Most pathologists wear rubber gloves for dissecting cadavers, but not all. Some prefer bare hands. Your father was a bare-hands man. Although there was a risk, if he cut himself while handling a diseased organ, of acquiring whatever infection that organ harbored, he believed that rubber gloves interfered with his sense of touch and hence with the accurate interpretation of the pathology.

Upstairs on the surgical ward I was as aware as everybody else of the stink of the floater and it did nothing to relieve the cloud of gloom under which I had labored since the meeting with your mother in the Two Eagles. I couldn't accept that I wasn't going to see her again. I simply didn't believe it. We'd been tired and depressed, I told myself, we'd feel differently in a day or two. I also had the worry of Henry. So I shambled about the hospital with my hands plunged deep in my pockets, head bowed and shoulders slumped, a picture of dejection and a far cry from my usual brisk self. Perhaps, I suddenly thought, she was feeling the same, perhaps she too found it impossible to think of us not meeting again? I was making dressing rounds with Sister, going from patient to patient, taking off old bandages and putting on new ones. The work was straightforward, and my mind drifted as I snipped at soiled and bloody dressings with my bandage scissors. Perhaps I should telephone her at home? It was risky, but this was an emergency. I needed to see her. Ratcliff was obviously still at work, the smell rising from the basement was ample evidence of that.

I was wrong. Ratcliff was back at Plantagenet Gardens when the telephone rang. He had come home twenty minutes earlier and without announcing his presence gone straight into his study. He didn't want to see your mother immediately. There had been tension between them for days now, which neither had attempted to relieve. I would imagine that all he wanted, after dissecting a floater, was to have a drink and listen to a little Mozart. Then the phone had rung. He'd heard her pick it up upstairs. From an impulse that he did not attempt to resist he reached for the telephone on his desk and very gently took the receiver off the hook and brought it to his ear. He heard your mother saying it was impossible (what was impossible?) and a man's voice saying that he only wanted an hour, and he was so shocked that he replaced the receiver almost immediately. But he had heard two names. One was his own; the other was mine.

Dinner, I would guess, was a strained affair that night. Having recovered from the first impact of moral shock aroused by hearing his wife making illicit arrangements on the telephone, Ratcliff had probably had to consider carefully what he ought to do next. Your mother once told me that in his way he was a passionate man, but that he placed no value on the expression of passion outside those situations in which he felt it appropriate. It was appropriate in the context of marital sexuality, he thought. It was appropriate on occasion when one fought the necessary battles that a responsible professional life demanded. It was not appropriate in politics, nor was it appropriate in the situation in which he now found himself. So he had not gone storming upstairs to confront your mother with what he had heard. He had, instead, as a reasonable man, tried to think beyond his anger. The impulse to revenge must be discounted. The desire to punish her was no basis for action, and by the pure exercise of will he waited out the first turmoil of hurt and rage so that he could decide what was best. There was also, I believe, his reluctance to face the truth, to acknowledge the extent to which he'd failed your mother.

By the time he heard the bell for dinner he'd resolved to say nothing. I don't believe he wanted to abandon his marriage. And I think it more than likely that he applied to this unhappy situation his own principles of pathology. Function was being revealed by failure. The *pathos* was conditioning the *logos*. He could not live with your mother in a state of emotional estrangement anymore. For too long he'd allowed them to live parallel lives. This present dysfunction proved it. He would expend every effort to recover the health of his marriage, and he expected to succeed—hadn't he always succeeded in carrying out his intentions, once he had properly formulated them? He knew your mother (he thought), he knew her weakness, he understood her in ways she did not understand herself. So he thought. Or so, at any rate, I imagine him thinking.

So there they sat at dinner in that somber dining room, where only the ticking of the clock on the mantelpiece, and the clatter of cutlery, broke the charged silence between them. They were having fish. He asked her if she would like a game of chess after dinner, but she'd promised to go round and see Brenda for an hour. He nodded and said no more. Your mother did not linger for coffee, but excused herself and went upstairs to put on her hat. Ratcliff was in his study when she left the house ten minutes later. Perhaps it saddened him to think of her doing damage to their marriage. Perhaps it saddened him to think that he was in some way responsible for that unhappiness. But now it had become a problem, a difficult, delicate problem of erasing the source of the unhappiness, undoing the damage, and bringing her home again.

He telephoned Brenda, ashamed of himself, I daresay, for doing it, but doing it all the same. Brenda improvised bravely. Fanny had said she might drop in but she hadn't appeared yet. So she was in on it too, thought Ratcliff, as he replaced the receiver. Then he sank back in his armchair, pressed his palms together with his fingertips just touching his lips, and frowned. Edward. Edward. Where had he heard the name recently? Who had been talking to him about someone called Edward? Then he had it: Vincent Cushing. One of Vincent Cushing's people had sewn the end of his rubber glove into a patient's stomach: Edward Haggard. Good God, he knew the man! They'd even sat at the same dinner table, at Cushing's house! Haggard had been at the other end, making Fanny laugh all night!

Ratcliff telephoned St. Basil's. He asked if Dr. Haggard was on duty. Yes he was, but he wasn't on the ward. He'd gone out for an hour. Would he like to speak to Dr. McGuinness? No, said Ratcliff, that wouldn't be necessary.

I was walking with your mother down a deserted street of decaying Georgian houses behind the hospital. It was a cool evening. The sky was not black, rather that curious shade of dark blue that makes you think of the hour before dawn. Strips of cloud scudded across a gibbous moon like rags and streamers chasing some ghostly night parade. Your mother had linked her arm in mine, and drawn in close to me, pressing against me as we walked. I'd told her about Henry Bird, who lay unconscious in the hospital in Griffin Head, and just talking about my fear that I'd caused his illness made it seem absurd. "Probably an aneurysm," said your mother. "It was there in his brain long before you even met me." She was not angry that I'd broken my promise and telephoned her. She told me she liked it that I needed her. Ratcliff never needed her, she said, he was self-sufficient, always in control. He had never shown weakness. Why should this make her unhappy? It stifled her. His strength stifled and limited her, such that she felt needed only by her child, by you, and even you were slipping away from her now, slipping into manhood and all that went with it.

How sad she was that night, almost as if she knew what was about to happen, all the horror. I hadn't dared to ask her if she'd changed her mind, so I didn't know if we were going on as before, or if these were our last moments. We stopped beneath a lamppost. Cupping her cheeks in my hands, my fingers still smelling of antiseptic, I kissed her eyes and forehead and the tip of her nose and felt again the familiar, potent, unsteady wave come coursing through me and leave me trembling, for it was at times too much, what I felt for her. The streetlight bathed her features in a yellowy radiance, her parted lips, her eyes searching my face, the frown of anxiety and unhappiness. "Darling Edward," she murmured. We walked on. The scene is etched in my mind.

When she let herself back into the house the light in the study was on and the door was open. "Is that you?" Ratcliff called, and she paused in the doorway of the study. "How is Brenda?"

"Brenda's fine."

"And Anthony?"

"I didn't see Anthony."

"Like to sit down and have a drink?"

"I think I won't, Ratcliff. I'm going up."

"As you please."

Anger then, surely, a black surge of it that he must have controlled only with the utmost difficulty. She wouldn't even sit down and have a drink with him. But he did control it. He had determined the course of action he would follow, and he was not going to sabotage it with rash outbursts, no matter what the provocation.

At this point, of the three of us, only Ratcliff fully understood what we were moving toward, only he knew that these in a sense were the last days. Your mother must have suspected, but we'd parted on a somewhat ambivalent note. As for me, what was about to happen, what Ratcliff was about to do, would come as the most violent of shocks, and have the most far-reaching of consequences—I feel them to this day.

Oh God.

So was this why you abandoned me, was this why you renounced me, threw me over, left me broken, in *all* senses broken—shunned, ignored, wretched, friendless, alone? Surely not, surely you would not so easily surrender what we had, yet you did, you allowed him to drive a wedge between us—!

Oh God.

He called you into the study again, didn't he? Isn't that how it happened? He called you in—you didn't want to see him then, he'd already hinted to you that he'd found out, and I imagine Brenda had telephoned by this time and told you about his calling her—so you must have known what was up. He was standing by the fireplace. "What is it, Ratcliff?" you said, and you avoided his eye as you crossed the room to the cigarette case on the low table, and busied yourself there. You were in gray that evening, the gray dress of soft wool, long-sleeved and tightly belted at the waist, which I loved—you moved across the room in that clingy dress, that sheath of gray wool, and stood frowning as you lit your cigarette and Ratcliff started in on you. *Why* did you give in to him? Oh, he is a man of strong will, I know, I've experienced the force of his personality, I've seen him storming down the corridors of St. Basil's so I do understand how intimidating he can be. But you are strong also! And didn't you think of me—that I was *with* you, and could give you all the support you might possibly need? All you had to do was stand firm in front of him for those few minutes, defy the man, refuse to crumble before his inquisition—why, why, my darling, need that have been so difficult, when you *knew* I was waiting, and you *knew* the strength of my commitment—? But you did. You allowed him to overwhelm you, and though I have been shattered and destroyed by this I bear no anger toward you. You were not strong enough—I understand. He told you he knew you weren't at Brenda's; he was bluffing, but you weren't to know this.

Oh God—

Oh God, not you, darling boy, your *mother!* Your *mother!* Oh my angel, my precious boy—

I have a picture in my mind of your mother coming into your bedroom, late at night, and you sitting at your table with a lamp focused on the model aeroplane you're building, and her standing there in the doorway, smoking, her dark form framed by the light from the upstairs landing, watching, silently, as with slim precise fingers you delicately assemble a wing—

Flight—how you loved flight—

And do you remember the evenings we had in Elgin? When we talked of ideas like the spirit, and the higher will, and service? And the quest for the infinite? You'd come after evening surgery, perhaps share the cold supper Mrs. Gregor had left, then we'd go upstairs. I'd read to you in the study, or we'd simply talk. Often we wouldn't turn the lights on, we'd watch the sunset smoldering on the horizon, burnishing the lip of the sea. I'd offer you a drink, but generally you refused. Oh, there was something in the atmosphere of that large, empty house, with the last glow of sunset, the gloom, the poetry we'd shared—a coming together of influences that was intoxicating for both of us, do you remember? I once told you facetiously after we'd read a little Swinburne together that we were bound to win the war because we were so much crueler than the Germans, and when (a little bewildered I suspect!) you asked me why I thought so, I clapped shut the Swinburne, waved it in the air, and cried: "That's why!" That made you laugh, didn't it!

Oh, and I'd pace the room, I'd limp up and down, talking of this and that—in a certain sort of mood, with a certain sort of listener, and among my own books, I'm the kind of man

who can talk for hours on end without once repeating himself,
or failing to entertain, and you of course know how to listen,
I always appreciated that in you, and listen you did, you gave
me the sympathetic ear I needed, you encouraged me to wan-
der, intellectually, from topic to topic, and occasionally, inevitably, I'd drift into areas of purely personal concern. I
remember once showing you a picture I was particularly fond
of, a reproduction of a romantic painting of a heap of icy debris
in an empty polar vastness, and telling you that landscape was
a state of the soul; and when you looked doubtful I said
painting should never be an act of imitation but rather a refusal
to imitate, because art, after all, must finally aspire to passion—and you said, "Passion?"

I paused in my pacing, I limped to the window and gazed
out. "She believed it was the best we were capable of," I
murmured, "civilized human beings."

"Who did?"

This was asked in the softest of tones, it was the merest
breath from the shadows. I said nothing. I leaned my forearm
on the window sash, then leaned my forehead against my arm,
and allowed my weight to rest on my good leg as I looked out
at the sea, from which the last of the sunset had by this time
vanished entirely. Neither of us broke the silence. You knew
who I was talking about. I said this. You said, "She thought
there was nothing better than passion? Physical passion?"

The moral asceticism of youth. "I don't think it was quite
as simple as that," I said, turning from the window and facing
you across the darkness. "I don't think you should judge her
harshly."

"She never wanted me to fly," you said. You were all in
shadow at the far end of the room, in an old high-backed wing
chair of Peter Martin's. "She tried to convince me there
wouldn't be a war."

"She loved you," I said. "She wanted to protect you. It's
a mother's natural instinct."

"I asked her if she was against fascism. She said of course she was, but she was against war too."

"And?"

"I said she couldn't be against both of them."

It suddenly came to me, and with devastating clarity, that I was losing you. That after tonight you would never come back. You'd reached some sort of decision about your mother and the part I'd played in her life, and there was no more you wanted to know, even though I had barely begun the task of explaining it to you. "I don't think she really understood what was at stake," you said, and for the first time I heard in your voice, and in your thinking, the unmistakable tone of Ratcliff, and my heart sank. The idea that you would carry with you, perhaps for the rest of your life, Ratcliff's idea of her, and his contemptuous dismissal of our love affair and all that it meant—it was unthinkable. I flailed about in my mind for some means, any means, to prevent this happening. "Did your father talk to you about her illness?" I said.

I saw you turn toward me in the gloom. A pause.

"Why do you ask?"

"I wish I could have seen her, that's all."

"But why?"

I gave a slight shrug and turned back toward the window—oh, I had promised myself never to bring this up with you, but I was desperate, desperate not to lose you! "It's nothing," I murmured. "These cases—these obscure kidney conditions—they're complicated. Tricky to diagnose properly."

Again a pause. "You think she was diagnosed wrongly?"

"No no no. No, I'm sure everything was done that could be done. I'd have liked to examine her myself, that's all."

What did you make of this? I couldn't tell; you were of course far too delicate to impute to me a dishonorable motive. Silently the moments passed, and I hated myself for what I was doing—sowing a seed of unease, this was what I was doing, planting suspicion in you, suspicion that would only fester until it brought you to me again.

You rose to leave soon afterwards, troubled, I could see, by our conversation but unsure just why. I shook your hand at the front door, and you were always so sweet when you left me, rather formal, rather apologetic for having taken so much of my time. As if I had anything better to do! You mounted your bicycle, and I watched you wobble off down the drive in the dusk, wheels crunching on the gravel, small and slim and upright in the saddle. Just where the drive turns out onto the coast road you turned to wave and you saw me there in my black corduroy jacket and snowy white shirt, a silk cravat at my throat, and I lifted a hand, standing in the doorway of my dark, soaring, narrow house, then turned and went inside and closed the front door behind me, and so into the surgery to see to Spike. All this, of course, before our relationship became one of doctor and patient.

Doctor and patient . . . I am aware, at times, of the grandeur of my spirit. At such times I find it absurd that it is housed in this puny frame, which has become, since Spike, a ruin. This is why I fell in love with Elgin, it offered a structure adequate to me, for I am not a small man *spiritually*. It is a jest of nature and an irony of circumstance that I am trapped in this flawed and puny frame, though never, I think, has it been brought home to me so clearly, until I met you, or rather, until you began to suffer your peculiar glandular disturbance, just how far this tendency in nature for botch and error can go. For my concern that you understand the nature of my relationship with your mother was soon to be overshadowed by my concern for *you*, for you and what started happening to you as you continued daily to face violent death.

My last real encounter with your father occurred as I emerged, one afternoon, into the hospital lobby from the basement stairs, hard by the bench where your mother and I had made love. He was in a dark green leather apron under his white coat, about to descend. He stopped dead and glared at me.

I believe the sight of me enraged him. I believe he had worked himself into such a state of jealous rage he was unable to control himself. He seized me by the arm. He called me an odious worm. He said I was furtive, insidious and contemptible. He said I couldn't begin to understand the mischief I was creating, the harm I was doing: all this he hissed at me in a low voice that attracted no one's attention, a cigar between his teeth, all the while gripping my upper arm so hard I couldn't get away from him. It was when he accused me of harming your mother that I made my retort, and given what I've told you, you will understand that I acted with restraint, much good it did me. All I said was, words to the effect that it was *he* who'd harmed her, and that he wasn't worthy of her. He fell silent. He let go of my arm and turned away, then suddenly turned back and with a sort of vicious swatting motion he slapped me with the back of his hand, very hard. The speed of the attack took me completely by surprise. I am a small man, and it knocked me off balance. My spectacles flew off. I remember thinking, in that first fraction of an instant when the mind operates with a sort of mad clarity, that I could regain my balance by flailing my arms about. So with white coat flapping, and stethoscope leaping wildly off my chest, and canting steeply backward, I windmilled there at the top of the stairs, but to no avail. I fell badly and hit the landing halfway down.

Of the fall itself I have no memory. One moment I stood flailing at the top of the staircase, the next I was lying in a heap on the landing, and when I tried to move there flared in my hip pain such as I had never before experienced, and would never have thought possible. Even as I lay there, nauseous, unwilling to attempt the smallest movement lest it bring back the pain, I was perfectly aware of what had happened, I had a clear picture of the pathology, it was quite obvious, really, after a fall like that: the neck of the femur was fractured. I'd broken my hip.

I suppose I must have passed out then. A dim awareness of faces and voices, of being loaded onto a stretcher, carried upstairs, and everything that jarred the hip had me crying out with pain. It wasn't until I was on a bed that someone gave me a shot of morphia and then, mercifully—nothing. The last thought I had, as the needle went in, was the phrase "pin and traction."

A broken hip is pretty straightforward. You open it up, dissect away the muscle, and bang in a steel pin. It's called a Smith-Petersen, and it holds the broken ends together. During cold weather, or when I'm tired, or if I've been on my feet too long, it'll produce inflammation in the femuro-pelvic joint, where the neck of the thighbone fits into the pelvis. Then it hurts like the devil, and that's when I need a shot of morphia to keep me cheerful—you know how I am when Spike's not behaving. And if it hadn't been for your father knocking me down the stairs that day I'd never have known the pleasure of Spike's company.

The ironies began crowding in on me thick and fast now. Not least among them was being admitted to St. Basil's as a patient, and then being assigned to a bed on my own surgical ward, with McGuinness my attending physician. It was a Nightingale ward, fifteen beds down either side of a long, high-ceilinged room, each with the patient's fever chart attached to a clipboard and dangling from a hook at the foot of the bed. The floors were parquet, and squeaked, the walls were painted pale green to shoulder height, white above, and there were three large windows down each wall with potted plants on the sills. The smell of antiseptic permeated everything. It was a busy place, patients shuffling about in dressing gowns, being wheeled off for this test or that—nurses running up and down—ward rounds morning and evening, when McGuinness would move from bed to bed with Sister—and twice a week grand rounds with Cushing himself.

God how I came to dread the sound of his footsteps as he

came clattering upstairs from the senior common room! I'm well aware of the attitude surgeons hold toward fracture patients, they're a nuisance, frankly, tedious and time-consuming and not very interesting. They need X-rays, cast changes, adjustments in traction, there are always a thousand small things to be done for them, and you can never relax, for although pinning a hip is the most common procedure on fracture service, once you've started the operation the chances of infection increase in almost direct proportion to the length of time the incision is open. The body will tolerate the pin only as long as there's no infection around it, so if infection does set in it can't be cleared until the pin is removed, and then you have to start all over again. So you must get it right first time and pretty quickly too. Cushing took a sort of grim relish in pointing all this out to me.

But the dominant feature of the period immediately after your father attacked me was the pain. Cushing operated the next day, whistling Puccini throughout, I'm told, and then I was put in traction, my leg suspended from the knee with weights attached to the ankle to stop the muscles pulling the pin out of alignment. The pain began with each return to consciousness, built rapidly to a peak, where it held with such excruciating intensity it had me twisting from side to side doing everything I could to keep from screaming, and not always succeeding. McGuinness would be sent for (it all seemed to take forever), but when he finally appeared, and made his way down the ward to me, rather than feel relief at his approach I would grow ever more frantic and by the time he reached my bed I'd literally be *begging* for the needle, and not even the twitch of contempt in his face could silence me, that's how bad it was.

Oh, never presume to judge the severity of another's pain! Never presume to judge what can be borne—dear boy, I need hardly tell *you* this. McGuinness would sit at my bedside, frowning, as he drew the fluid into the barrel of the syringe, and he'd murmur: "Calm down, man, you'll get your shot"—

and even in my bleary wretchedness I could read his mind, he was thinking it contemptible that a man (and a doctor) should humiliate himself like this on a public ward. I didn't care. I just wanted the needle. At last I'd feel the prick, then the prickle, then I'd begin to sweat, my mouth would go dry, the pain would ease, and I'd lie there, soaked in sweat, gazing up at the Balkan frame of steel bars and pulleys over the bed, and in the now misty remnants of consciousness I'd breathe a prayer of thanks. Soon I'd drift into a shallow, restless sleep.

I gaze out over the airfield now and try to shake off the shame that clings to the memory of those days. It was terrible, terrible—the indignity of being dependent on the nurses for bowel and bladder functions. Being unable to turn over in bed, or reach for a book or a cigarette. Crumbs getting into the sheets. But worst of all, the pain. I tried to keep the injections down to two a day but I always needed more. I tried to control it—I bore it as best I could—but when it began truly to bite, when it climbed to that crest and simply *did not break*—then I'd feel my willpower loosen and shred like the fiber of an old rubber band. McGuinness would come, eventually, his face a mask of professional neutrality but I could see the pity and scorn it concealed. With wordless efficiency he'd give me my shot and after a moment or two the pain ebbed away, the lights grew brighter and I'd start to feel better, though curiously it wasn't that it disappeared, it was still there but it had lost the power to dominate consciousness to the exclusion of all else, it didn't matter, somehow, it didn't *hurt* anymore.

I'd know then a sense of expanding wonder; voices on the ward seemed to come from a thousand miles away, I'd think of your mother, and my heart would grow tender. Even then, you see, even in that utter extremity of suffering, she was with me, she was my inspiration, and I have come to believe that without her—without the knowledge that she was in the world, loving me—which I took on faith, she never visited me of course—without that, those early days would have been impossible. For I believe (Peter Martin taught me this) that spirit can be mobilized to a therapeutic end. My will to heal, to create a bony union in my femur, was in those first days grounded in the idea of your mother, so in a very real sense it was *through her* that I was able to inspire the resources of my body to fuse the fragments into a whole.

But they were strange and terrible, those days and nights in traction. I once awoke in darkness to the certainty that the wires of my Balkan frame were the spars and rigging of a ship, an eerie death ship about to cast off and carry me over a subterranean sea to some island of the dead from which I would never return. I struggled to get off the ship and in my panic managed to set the whole frame shaking, the whole complicated system of weights and pulleys, and in the process damn nearly tore Spike clean out of my hip. The night sister later told me that it was only with the greatest difficulty that they were able to subdue me and settle me down with a needle, for in my efforts to get off the ship I'd somehow found the strength of ten men.

When finally I was allowed out of bed, and started hobbling up and down the ward on crutches, I was a gaunt, gray, hollow-eyed creature, listless and ill-tempered, prone to headaches and itching and sudden waves of pain—and my hair was shot through with this wild streak of white. Because of the pain, and the morphia injections I had to have to control it, my arms were like pincushions, the punctures crowded together in rashes. I'd already been told that Henry Bird was dead, which did little to help, but as I say, at this stage I still believed in your mother, and remembered our last conversation, when she'd so deftly dispelled my feelings of guilt about him. I was even able to handle the shock of having Vincent Cushing come and tell me quite bluntly that I wouldn't be required on his service any longer. Even this I could cope with, for I'd already anticipated Ratcliff talking to him, urging my dismissal—and getting his way, for of course he shared with Cushing a near-impregnable position high in the hierarchy of St. Basil's. The shame of it was, of course, that I couldn't say a word in my own defense. I couldn't accuse him of knocking me down the stairs, because that would have dragged your mother into it, which was unthinkable. But yes, I could cope with it, because I thought she loved me, believed in me, and was waiting for me.

I was in traction for six weeks, and it was another six weeks before I was able to bear weight on the leg. I changed. During those terrible weeks, I changed. The gaunt gray man who limped out of St. Basil's in the summer of 1938 was a very different creature from the passionate fellow who'd stood his ground that spring and told the senior pathologist what harm he was doing his wife. Suffering leaves its mark; what is it Wordsworth says?

> Suffering is permanent, obscure and dark,
> And shares the nature of infinity.

My suffering was certainly permanent; as to its darkness and obscurity, your mother's rejection was the single worse shock I had to bear—all of it I could have endured without faltering, had she remained true. She did not; and though my love did not abate in the slightest—it grew stronger, in fact—I was forced to go forward alone. This tempered me. It matured me. I aged many years in those short weeks, learned much about the spirit and about that pear-shaped, fist-sized, four-chambered bag we call the human heart. Poetry, you see, was my great aid, in those dark nights, to know that what I was experiencing had been experienced before, and by men who could transmute that experience into beauty:

> Most wretched men
> Are cradled into poetry by wrong;
> They learn in suffering what they teach in song.

James, fallen angel: this is my song.

• • •

I still possess the letter she sent me. I'd intended one day to show it to you, but I don't suppose it matters now. It was shattering. I believe it would have devastated me even if I'd been in rude good health. It would have devastated any man. It didn't say much. We were never to see each other again. I was to keep my promise not to try and make her change her mind. It could never work for us—surely, she wrote, I must have known that? She had a son, a home, a marriage. It was over. No tenderness. No word of love. The first time I read it was like being struck full force in the face with a bucket of cold seawater. Spike started up immediately, and I had to shout for McGuinness though he'd seen to me only an hour before. What was I to do? What could I do? I smelled the hand of Ratcliff all over that letter. It was all too easy to imagine her situation: he would answer the telephone, intercept the mail, watch her like a hawk; any attempt on my part would only make things worse. I wasn't afraid of Ratcliff, don't think that. Despite what he'd done to me, don't think that. But I was afraid of what he might do to your mother, should I disobey her instructions.

I did on one occasion telephone her. It was the middle of the afternoon, so Ratcliff was almost certainly down in Pathology. I made my way on crutches to the end of the ward and the public telephone. In my dressing gown and slippers, and weak with pain and apprehension, I dialed the number. It was picked up on the fourth ring. "Yes?" she said. How flat her voice was. Devoid of expression, achingly, pathetically empty of feeling—this was what he'd brought her to. "It's me," I said, "can you talk?"

"Who is it?"

"Edward."

"Oh." A long pause. Then: "Yes?"

"I got your letter. I know you didn't mean it."

"I'm afraid I can't talk to you," she said in that cold, dead voice, and hung up the receiver. She was sealed off from me, in some grim prison of Ratcliff's making. The next afternoon a rather sinister thing happened. Lying on my bed I realized that he was standing at the end of the ward in a black rubber apron with his sleeves rolled up, staring straight at me. Then he was at my bedside! "You little fool, she doesn't want you," he hissed, "don't you understand that? *She doesn't want you!*" I tried to raise my head from the pillow but could not—the effort exhausted me—I was drenched in sweat—a wave of nausea swept over me—and when I opened my eyes again he was gone. She'd told him, then. I didn't try to reach her again.

Oh, I thought about it. I thought for a time it was my duty to reach her, to somehow get her away from Ratcliff and make her see what he was doing to her; I couldn't forget the tone of her voice when she'd said, "I'm afraid I can't talk to you." They echoed in my head, those dead flat tones, during the pain-racked days and nights I spent in St. Basil's, they devastated me, and it was a week before I finally began to attempt to accept the fact that I had to let her go. I have to let her go, I have to let her go: up and down the ward I'd hobble on my crutches, the words like the chant of a mob in my head, you have to let her go, you have to let her go—armies marching across Europe, and as they marched they chanted, you have to let her go, you have to let her go. "But I *cannot* let her go!"—I awoke one night with this scream on my lips, and woke the ward (what's worse I woke Spike too), but it did no good, those marching armies just kept on and on: you have to let her go, you have to let her go.

Eventually I was discharged from St. Basil's. I was getting about with just the aid of a stick by this time; the pain was still bad, and the scuffed leather medical kit I carried containing needle and ampoules was, if not the center of my existence, certainly necessary for my sense of security. I'd accepted the inevitable, and felt as though a loved one had died: I was in a state of mourning. My interest in the outside world was nil, and I was incapable of activity. I spent my days and nights shuffling wretchedly about my room in Jubilee Road, glancing into volumes of poetry only to toss them aside with weary indifference. I knew I would never love again. I would never do anything again. All I could do was grieve.

I told myself to forget her, but I thought about her constantly. Everything reminded me of her. The lamps. The rug. The fly-in-glass in my trouser pocket—I kept it over on Spike's side, they somehow seemed connected, Spike and the fly. I'd take it out a dozen times a day and turn it in my fingers till the sobs came, till the grief racked me anew, and that would get Spike going, and I'd have to reach for the scuffed leather medical kit to deal with the pain, for the one pain unfailingly engendered the other, as though a current flowed from heart to hip, and hip to heart. The Keats she gave me, which we'd read from together in front of the fire—it was practically crystalline with associations, as was the porcelain vase, the flowers (I never let Mrs. Kelly throw out her flowers)—dead now, these many weeks, and their water stinking, but I gathered the brittle fallen petals in a saucer and gazed at them for hours on end: *for she had touched them!* Her voice was in my dreams, though I hardly slept at all, but the semi-conscious daze I'd slip into, after relieving Spike—it was then that I was most susceptible to her presence, the sound of her voice, her footfall on the landing outside my door—I'd heave up out of my chair at dead of night, and with the grotesque gait, part limp, part lurch, of the agitated cripple, haul myself over to the door and fling it wide and there'd be—nothing!

Nothing. I sank deeper into listless depression. It occurred to me that if I brought up the memory of every occasion on which we'd been together—what we'd done, what we'd said—I could somehow rob them of their power to ravage and devastate me. I could defuse them. It did no good. Worse: it exacerbated the pain, which got Spike going, so I'd have to have a shot, and then I'd hear her, and so it started all over again.

I was going mad.

I had to do something—good Good, I had to make a living! I forced myself to face facts. A career in surgery was no longer a possibility, so I had to think about general medicine. Positions in London were few, but I could easily enough find work as an assistant in some country practice and make five hundred pounds a year. And given all that had happened, given my state of mind, the idea of getting out of London actually roused, for the first time in weeks, a small faint flicker of interest—until, that is, the reality of country practice came home to me. Was this really the best I could hope for? The promising young doctor who'd won a coveted place at one of the great London teaching hospitals—was I now to become an overworked, underpaid assistant to some country doctor? It rather looked as though I was.

This provoked fresh despair, lassitude, self-reproach. I was worthless and despicable, and I deserved all the misfortune that had befallen me. I had never been anything but worthless and despicable, and it was impossible that your mother could ever have loved me. She was right to reject me. I was incapable of love, I was incapable of achieving anything of value, I was petty, narcissistic, dishonest, weak, and my one sole aim had always been to hide my weakness—this seemed undeniably true, for apparently I was now addicted to morphia as well. It only surprised me that I should have had to be brought so low to recognize it.

The salient feature of those days, then, a profound dissatisfaction with myself which, when it became particularly acute, set off Spike, which then had me reaching for my medical kit, and in the brief dreamy hours of release that followed your mother would become vividly present to me, which would set the whole sorry train in motion once more.

The dead, flat creature caught in a prison, and powerless to escape, was not, I then realized, your mother—it was me. No wonder she rejected me. Such were my thoughts. And any pity I may have felt for her, should, I saw, in justice, have been directed toward myself: it was *I* who was weak and powerless! Thus I railed at myself, thus did I make myself suffer, and in the process derived a sick, self-punitive gratification. It occurred to me at one point that if I died your mother would then, at least, be forced to acknowledge what I'd felt for her, and what she had sacrificed. Oh, I was an open wound, and without sleep I could not heal.

I realized that the first thing was to get off the morphia. Spike hurt, this was a fact of life, even after bony union was effected in my hip; and he hurt worst as I fell off to sleep, when my muscles relaxed and the damaged bone ground like a drill against its seating in the pelvis. A needle relieved that hurt, not only relieved it but brought in its train waves of peace and serenity—nonetheless I couldn't use morphia as a crutch for the rest of my life, with God knows what effect upon my moral and intellectual functioning. So I stopped. One morning I just stopped.

At first all was well. I had risen at my usual time and gone without my morning shot, and spent the next hours looking at the newspaper. It was around noon—twelve hours after the last injection—that I began to grow uneasy. I became aware that a feeling of weakness had gradually crept over me. I began to yawn, then noticed that I couldn't stop shivering. I pulled a blanket round my shoulders. I seemed to be weeping, though not out of misery, it wasn't true weeping, it was, rather, a hot, watery discharge that had begun pouring from my eyes and nose in a copious stream. I crawled into bed—that huge creaky bed I had shared so often with *her!*—and fell into a restless sleep.

Throughout that warm summer afternoon I tossed and

turned under the sheet and was tormented by grotesque dreams. I saw Ratcliff bearing down on me in his black rubber apron, his face a rictus of rage and in his hand an amputation knife. I found myself on the steel table in the postmortem room with Ratcliff and Miggs and Cushing sniggering down at me. My thorax was open, my insides were piled neatly on my chest, and my penis was rolling around on the floor. I got up on one elbow, concerned to recover my penis, and my insides slithered off and fell on the floor and they all laughed.

I awoke at six in the evening: eighteen hours since the last injection. I couldn't stop yawning—I yawned so violently I feared I would dislocate my jaw. Armies of ants crawled about under my skin. Huddled in my blanket with the tears pouring from my eyes, and a watery mucus from my nose, I managed with difficulty to smoke a cigarette. I was shivering uncontrollably. At one point I struggled to the fireplace and peered at myself in the mirror. My pupils were dilated and the skin of my face was pimpled like gooseflesh. Suddenly I felt violently sick. There was no time to reach the bathroom down the hall, I had to make do with my chamber pot. The vomiting was explosive. Its contents were streaked with blood. Kneeling there over my bloody flux I opened my shirt and saw the skin of my belly knotted and corrugated as though a nest of vipers were writhing beneath it. Diarrhea soon followed. But I did not crack.

The hours crawled by. I called your mother's name, it gave me strength. I was doing it for her, this was the only way I could go on with it. By the next morning I was in truly pitiful condition. In a desperate attempt to relieve the chills racking me I had gone back to bed and covered myself with every blanket I could lay my hands on. My whole body shook and twitched beneath this mountain of bedclothes, though the pain not only in my hip but in all my muscles prevented me from getting sleep or even rest. I clambered out of bed and for a while I limped back and forth across the room, attempting to get warm. I opened a book and tried to read; hopeless of course. With tears of frustration and misery I climbed back into bed: the sheets and blankets were soaked through to the mattress. Then came a knock at the door! Filthy, unshaven, befouled with vomit, I called through the door: "Who is it?" My voice was a weak, fluty thing, like an old man's. I was only just able to keep the concerned Desmond Kelly from coming in to see what was the matter.

Time passed with excruciating slowness, and no relief came. I could neither eat nor drink, and in the course of that second day I became weaker and weaker as my bodily reserves were consumed and vitality slipped away. I thought then that unless I found relief I would surely die; and that seemed a heavy price to pay for dispensing with a crutch. Shortly after noon I broke. I cracked. I barely had the energy to drag myself out of my armchair and with trembling fingers make up a needle. But thirty minutes later (so rapid was my recovery) I was downstairs, shaved, clean, and joking weakly with Desmond Kelly about the terrible noises he'd heard from my room in the night. Eight hours after that I felt again the unease that had ushered in the nightmare, and I decided to prolong my holiday from hell. As I have ever since.

Three days later there again came a knock at the door. It was early evening and the light was starting to go. Desmond Kelly stood there with a letter. I tore it open. It was from Hugh Fig, the solicitor in Griffin Head. Apparently Henry's will had been read: everything was left to me, including the house. I looked up—gazed with a dawning smile into the mild, sad face of Desmond Kelly—and in that moment knew I was saved. In the midst of my darkness had come this one pure blessed shaft of grace. Despite all I'd done to him, Henry had kept faith with me. Grace, unbidden, had entered in, and my next steps were obvious, certain, and natural.

I felt my vital energies rekindled—I felt I could act again! I said this to Desmond Kelly. "So you can, doctor," he said.

He wasn't surprised. A wave of euphoria rose within me. I seized him by the hand—a wild, mad fellow I surely appeared, gray-skinned and unkempt, my mood careering crazily from profound depression to violent excitement in the space of a moment. Desmond Kelly was imperturbable. He knew the human heart.

I decided to go down to Griffin Head without delay. I telephoned Hugh Fig and told him to expect me the following afternoon. He asked me if I wanted to stay in my uncle's house—*my* house, as it it now was. No, I told him, I would prefer not to; could he recommend a decent hotel? Oh, the Ship, he said, you'll want to stay in the Ship.

Late the following morning finds me threading my way through the crowds at Victoria with as much of a spring in my step as Spike will allow. The day was warm and I was in my linen suit, which I hadn't worn once that summer, having barely been out of the house and when I did go out having little concern for my appearance. Not so now! I was freshly shaved, I was wearing my good Panama, dark glasses to hide the shadows under my eyes—yet another sleepless night, though this time it was excitement that kept me up—and a light summer raincoat thrown about my shoulders. I had my stick, my ticket, my light traveling bag, and Spike was under control. I felt like a man on the threshold of a new life. I felt as though a great journey was beginning—as indeed it was, a journey that has led me to this moment, this airfield, this duty, this end—this oddly glorious end—

I bought a newspaper from a vendor in the station. The situation in Czechoslovakia was critical. I sat by the window, smoking cigarettes, my stick clasped between my legs, my bag on the overhead rack. How beautiful England looked that day! Glimpses of the Downs, lush green rolling hills with smooth humped backs, like burial mounds, and the sheep cropping at the grass in the sunlight. Fields of golden corn, a high blue sky and a warm sun, sleepy villages, great estates— what did I care for dark portents of war, those unknown people in that distant land? Then comes that exhilarating moment, the first smell of salt in the wind. You leave the hills and descend to the coastal plain, there's the lighthouse, the cliffs, the sea sparkling beneath that deep blue sky, and at last you're steaming into Griffin Head itself.

I took a taxi into town and after settling in at the Ship made my way to Hugh Fig's office on the front. We discussed the disposal of Henry's house, and the handsome portfolio of stocks he'd left. It was all quite straightforward. We concluded the business and then, just as I was about to leave, Fig asked me if I remembered Peter Martin. Of course I did, I told him. I'd talked to Peter Martin on the telephone several times during Henry's last illness. He was the GP. What Hugh Fig said next was to have a profound impact not only on my life but also, I believe, on yours. "Peter Martin," he said, "is an old man. He's frankly too old to handle the work by himself much longer. It occurred to me that you may know someone who'd be interested in buying the practice."

I paused, with my hand on the doorknob—and you know what happened next, I went up to Elgin and I fell in love with the house; I fell in love with the house and made of it a museum of nostalgia, a temple to the memory of your mother, where I worshiped her spirit and would undoubtedly have continued to do so had you not appeared and drawn me back into the stream of life. Was this why you came to me? Was this your purpose, to show me the possibility of a life after death? Of a reconciliation of spirit and nature? Of a *reunion*?

Though ever since our last conversation, when Ratcliff's tone was in your voice, I'd felt as if I was losing you—losing you as I'd once lost her! And the prospect had hit me harder than I'd ever have thought possible. So I'd sown my seed of unease. By raising a question about your mother's illness I had instilled a doubt in your mind that would, I hoped, eventually draw you back to Elgin. Not that your doubt would be ill-founded;

I had reflected often in the long watches of the night as to what occurred during the last weeks of your mother's life. Doctors are notoriously unreliable in the diagnosis and treatment of their own families, this is well established. How much more so, the doctor whose wife has deceived and betrayed him? Ratcliff Vaughan was a cruel, aggressive man—did he dismiss your mother's early symptoms (and in kidney disease these can be oddly oblique)—as "nerves"? Did he, consciously or otherwise, allow her to sicken, and all the while reassure her, and you, that nothing was really wrong? The diarrhea, the fatigue, the loss of skin tone—all just "nerves"? Did he punish her thus for betraying him? It is not inconceivable. So when I sowed my seed it was not out of sheer gratuitous mischief; I had serious grounds for suspicion.

For I'd seen her myself in the spring of '39, and nothing had been wrong with her then. A woman at a dinner party had thrown me into a storm of misery merely by mentioning her name—"Fanny!" she'd cried. "Don't you know Fanny?" That's what brought it on, that's what brought on the fever once more.

It was the day Hitler entered Prague. She wasn't expecting me. She wouldn't have seen me had she known I was coming. It was almost a year since the night we'd walked down an empty street behind the hospital, beneath a gibbous moon, . . . I'd driven up from Elgin after breakfast, reached London at noon, and parked under a budding chestnut tree on the other side of Plantagenet Gardens, having stopped at a telephone box a little earlier to establish that Ratcliff was in St. Basil's. I had no clear idea what I was going to do. Wait for her to come out, perhaps, or march up the steps and stand beneath the portico, between the pillars, and press the bell, stand there until the heavy black front door swung inward and admitted me to a house I had never entered before, a hallway with a polished wood floor, a large mirror over a side table—

I sat in the Humber smoking cigarettes and watching the

door. At one point a middle-aged woman in a shapeless brown coat came out with a basket over her arm and went off along the pavement. Now she is alone, I thought. I must still my racing heart, compose myself, get out of the car, cross the road, knock on the door—

It was at least half a minute before she opened it. "Edward," she said—not coldly, but with surprise, curiosity, a flicker of annoyance—then: "What happened to your hair?" I don't remember what I said. I had thought of her so often, since we last met, that actually to be with her paralyzed me. I remember in my confusion noticing the few fine wrinkles at the corners of her eyes—her skin was as clear and white as ever, her eyes still shone with liquid light, but I didn't remember those fine lines before. I think it may have been the sunshine. It was a bright day. What did she see? A ruin. "May I come in and talk to you?" I said.

A slight frown. "I suppose so."

She led me down the hall. Walking behind her had always aroused me, and it did so now. We went into a drawing room with aquamarine curtains, silk-shaded lamps, and richly patterned rugs on a gleaming wood floor. French windows were open at the far end, spilling sunlight into the room. On the coffee table stood a vase of flame-colored tulips. On the mantelpiece a silver cigarette box. She took one and lit it. "I can't give you any tea, I'm afraid," she said, "Iris has gone shopping."

"Yes, I saw her."

"Oh you did. Edward, what is it you want? It's really not very convenient to have you here."

The sense of transgressing was so strong I found it hard to speak. I am never articulate in situations of high emotion. "There's something you must know. It may make no difference to you at all, but I must tell you."

An intake of breath. She found this tedious. She found me a nuisance. A bore. This deflated me. I had not anticipated such coolness in her. I'd thought she might be angry, but not cool. Not bored. "Well?"

How to say it? How to make an impression on her? In a sense it didn't matter. I already knew it was hopeless. She would throw me out in a moment, but I was *with* her, and that was enough. Angry, indifferent, scornful—it hardly mattered. It was her. "It hasn't been easy for me. I haven't been able to forget you."

She was sitting on the sofa, half-turned toward the French windows, smoking, waiting. Not looking at me. A tissue of small sounds filled the room, a bird, a clock, a voice from another garden. What we call silence. "I have a practice on the south coast now," I said. "I have a house. I make a reasonable living." No response. I didn't say I have a morphia habit. "I live quietly, I do two surgeries a day and house calls in the afternoon." Nothing. Christ, what was I *saying?* "But I don't feel anything," I cried, "I can't take pleasure in anything, I'm not properly alive, all I know is you're not with me and all the rest is empty, useless, dead, without meaning—" I paused, and realized I was standing in front of her fireplace with my arms in the air, like a man giving a harangue. She was turned toward me now so I said, with all the love in my heart: "Won't you come and live with me?"

She frowned. She leaned over to stub out her cigarette then rose to her feet. She gazed into my eyes, shaking her head slightly, like a mother half-amused at the mischief of a favorite child. She took my hands in hers. "You shouldn't have come here," she said quietly. "It could be difficult for me. You didn't think of that, did you?"

I felt a fool. No, I hadn't thought of that. Blinded by the intensity of my feelings, I'd behaved clumsily, I'd made her life difficult. "I didn't think you'd let me see you otherwise."

"I probably wouldn't have."

She dropped my hands, turned away, sat down again on

the sofa. The sunlight from outside made a sort of gray gloom at this end of the room. "I'm sorry," I said.

"Sit down," she said. "Darling, what could have come of it? Really? All that secrecy. It became so wearying, telling lies. It drains one's vitality. It never adds up to anything. We just fanned the flames, and it was torment because we couldn't ever be together."

"But we were together!"

"Oh no we weren't. You must realize this. The only way of dealing with love is being together for a long time, the world shut out, being in bed together all night long, waking together in the morning. All we had was a furtive hour here or there—it was making us both miserable."

"But what could we do? You wouldn't leave Ratcliff."

"How do you know?"

"I asked you."

"You weren't very insistent."

"What do you mean?"

"You didn't try and take me from him."

"I'm trying now!"

She lifted her eyebrows. "Oh," she said, turning away again, "what good does talking do?" She rose from the sofa and walked down the room to the French windows, where she stood in the sunlight with her arms folded, gazing out into the garden. I came up behind her, slipped an arm round her waist and pressed myself against her. "Oh my love," I breathed, "my heart—"

"No, Edward." She deftly disengaged herself and moved away. "I think you'd better go now."

"What am I to do? Now you tell me I could have taken you from him!"

"Oh, maybe you could have, I don't know. We had an affair. It's over now. Go away—get on with your life—get on with somebody else. I'm sorry for what happened to you but there's no more I can do."

I sank into a chair and stared at the floor, elbows on my knees and hands dangling. Her words had devastated me. A moment later she pulled me gently to my feet. She gazed into my face with a worried, tender expression. "You're a sensitive man," she said, "I always loved that in you. You're a real doctor, Edward, and that's rare. Find someone to love. Please, darling."

I shook my head.

"You must."

The doorbell rang and we spun apart. The mood shattered, it was as if we were scrambling out of a pit of blackness, back into everyday life. She went out, closing the door behind her. "You see what I mean?" she said when she came back a few moments later, as I tried to take her hands again. "No, you must go now. Really, Edward, I insist. Go now. And please don't visit me again."

At the front door she took my face in her hands and kissed me softly for several seconds on the lips. Then she opened the door and I left. I sat smoking in the car. A little later I saw her go out; she did not see me. I did not follow her. I sat there all day and watched the house. She came home late in the afternoon. Night fell and a pale moon, like a claw, filtered its light down through the branches of the chestnut trees. I drove back down to Griffin Head feeling that I had done myself no good, that I had simply fueled the flames of my misery. But I gloried in the smell of her perfume on my fingers.

It was just after the declaration of war that I learned of her death. It came as a dreadful shock. It was a Saturday, and I was alone in the house when the letter from McGuinness arrived in the afternoon post. I stood there in the hallway with the letter in my hand and then for some reason I turned and limped down the passage to the kitchen. Mrs. Gregor had washed the dishes and stacked them beside the sink on a kitchen towel, and rather than use a second towel to spread them out on—how odd that I should remember this, of all things—she had made an unsteady pyramid of cups and plates and glasses and cutlery that even as I looked at it seemed to tremble and be on the point of collapsing. The floor was swept and the table was clear apart from a little heap of eggshells, potato peelings and other organic rubbish in the middle of a sheet of brown paper. This puzzled me; not being a gardener I took a few moments to realize that this heap of rubbish was compost for the garden, my first thought was of some kind of offering.

I went out into the scullery and looked at the Wellington boots and watering cans and piles of yellowing newspapers, and then I went outside and walked down the garden and through the gate and so down the path to the edge of the cliff. The light was just beginning to go. I stood and gazed out at autumn sunlight on a calm sea, seeing how it spilled onto the surface in a great broad swathe made up of countless shards and scraps of light, closely packed at the center so as to form a dense blanket of silver and only at the edges breaking into its constituent fragments. The difficulty somehow lay in understanding the activity of the light on the water, in iden- tifying a pattern in the constant movement of the waves, the endless dancing and shifting as the current lifted the blanket of light and then rolled on, leaving it to settle once more— thus does the stricken mind clutch at distraction.

How long I stood there I don't know. After a while I became aware that long washes of pale blue and mauve were angling into the splotchy molten mess of golden radiance where the sun was going down while above it, high and flecky, its point to the west, an arrowlike cloud formation had appeared. After some minutes the mauve and blue bands turned a smoldering pink which grew deeper in tone as the sun touched the horizon and then went down. I seemed to awaken at that point, and as dusk rapidly descended I made my way back up the path to the house. Into the scullery I came and slammed the back door behind me—and heard a frightful crash from the kitchen. Mrs. Gregor's pile of dishes had fallen off the counter and shattered on the floor. I stood gazing in horror at the mess and then fled limping to the surgery. It was nephritis, McGuinness said. Kidney failure. She was ill for some weeks and then sank rapidly. She died in St. Basil's. Nothing anybody could do.

I attended the funeral. The ghastly echo of that other occasion, the day I first saw her—saw her and knew her and loved her! For the church was the same—many of the mourners were the same—and yes, I arrived late—but not accidentally this time, not because I'd been up all night in Accident and Casualty, but because I didn't think I'd be welcome. I slipped into the back of the church after the service had begun. A few heads turned, a few familiar faces—the Cushings were there, McGuinness, the Piker-Smiths. What was different though was the presence of so many uniforms. Almost all the men were in uniform and quite a few of the women (not me of course, Spike kept me from active service). Ratcliff had joined the RAMC, and from the partial glimpse I had of him up at the front of the church he looked, in khaki, more aggressive than ever. English funerals I've never found particularly conducive to grief but this one was. For me. Not for anyone else that I was aware of, but for me. I wept throughout, noiselessly, without once attempting to stanch the flow and careless of the opinion of my neighbors. I stood there with my hat in my hand, my stick hooked over the pew in front, and allowed the tears to course freely down my face.

How good it is for the heavy heart to weep! I have wept often for your mother, in varying moods and circumstances, but never I think have I been as cleansed and refreshed and *emptied* by my tears as I was at her funeral: I voided my grief, that day. I had been in shock you see, ever since I learned of her death, and had failed fully to acknowledge that grief. Now it came pouring out of me in a hot, steady stream that continued to flow even as her coffin was borne slowly down the aisle to the strains of the *Dies Irae*. Oh, it cut me like a knife to see her coffin, to think of her pale perfect body — no, not perfect, not perfect at all anymore, diseased, rather, spoiled and diseased—but I could not tear my eyes away, I gazed with mounting horror as it was borne down the aisle toward me—and then I saw you.

I saw you. Or I saw, rather, among the coffin-bearers, a young man in the uniform of an RAF pilot-officer, recently commissioned and wearing his wings. A small man, delicate of feature, his dark head lowered in grief—I knew this must be her son, and I found myself staring at you with a fierce intentness, so fierce an intentness, in fact, that you sensed it, and lifted your head, and stared, for an instant, straight into my eyes—straight into my *soul!*—before dropping your head once more. You don't remember the look we exchanged that day; I have never forgotten it. The afternoon you came to my surgery and said: "I believe you knew my mother"—I remembered it then, for there was, in your face, in the church that day, an expression of feeling that precisely and exactly mirrored my own. I felt between us a current of communication, and when soon afterwards I slipped away (I did not linger long among the mourners) this was what I carried away with me, the memory of meeting your gaze and finding replicated in it my own passionate experience of grief and loss. No, you may not consciously remember it, nonetheless it formed the foundation of the friendship we erected round her memory, like a tabernacle round a host—

But that didn't happen for months. First would come the winter, and oh, such coldness I remember that winter! It was the fiercest in forty years and we certainly felt it in Elgin. The generator broke down repeatedly and the wind howled in round those warped old window frames, so we had to close up most of the house and put in paraffin heaters. The rooms on the seaward side, including my study, were too cold to be used, though I still liked to go in late at night, in my overcoat, and for an hour or two watch wild seas hammering at the cliff. Mrs. Gregor had seen many winters in Griffin Head but none as bad as this, she said.

Whenever I had the chance I went down to the lonely, bird-haunted wastes of Elder Harbour, a large natural inlet created by inroads of the sea, from which the tide ebbed through a channel in the shingle beach, leaving marsh, mud flats and small streams. The wind howled about me as I trudged along, gulls dipped and screamed overhead, beneath lowering gray clouds, and the smell in the wind was of salt and rank fish and cord grass. Mrs. Gregor had told me about a great gale-driven tide that had swept across the marsh flats one winter when she was a child, flooded a farm on the other side of the coast road and drowned all the pigs. The ruin of an old wind-mill loomed at the desolate western end, much of the brick-work crumbled on its seaward face, and within the spars and ribs of the sails the latticework was splintered and smashed. The shaft no longer turned. In this mill the local kidney rock was once ground for cement, and on the sands nearby I came upon scattered lumps of the stone, grayish and finely grained and laced with translucent yellow veins composed of calcite crystals that for some reason struck me as beautiful, and which I collected and brought back to Elgin. I kept one on my desk in the surgery, and an old man told me that the cement it yielded was so hard that modern drills wore out on it and paint would stick for only a short time even if a sticky surface was applied first. Dead. Dead. But there could be no end (I thought), it was not the living woman I loved but her spirit, and that was unchanged and unchangeable. What is the life of the body against the life of the spirit? All too easy to see her flesh a pile of rank matter heaving with worms, not only her, all of us, you, me, all of us. Life is a squalid little farce if it offers no higher meaning than this—?

I continued to function, morning surgery, rounds after lunch, evening surgery, on call at night. It was a cold winter and Spike was vicious. My need of morphia to control the pain was at times intense, but never did it interfere with the conscientious discharge of my duty. I am a man of robust character and never permitted my judgment or competence to be impaired. Nonetheless that winter my need was acute, and I was forced to raise my dosage and shift from intramuscular to intravenous injection for quicker effect. I kept a supply of the drug in the surgery, in a cupboard under lock and key. An inspector from the Home Office did drop by, unannounced, one morning, but the books were quite in order. In fact—as I was quick to point out to him—I prescribed a good deal of morphia to my patients, the practice including many elderly persons among whom cancer was common. The tolerance for morphia of patients like these—Nan Hale-Newton was a case in point—increased (I told him) over time, and often quite rapidly: it was not rare that a quarter-grain dosage would have to be raised to three grains within a matter of weeks. For this reason I always had to have a large supply on hand, and the man from the Home Office was satisfied that no illicit prescription was occurring.

January was a month of gales, high winds, and angry seas, and Elgin was battered continually by storms. One wild night I heard glass breaking overhead, and went up to the top floor to investigate. There were rooms up there that I hadn't visited since the days I was first in the house, rooms in which Peter Martin still had furniture stored. Only one light worked, on the landing. I limped along the dusty creaking boards and into each of the rooms, where sheeted furniture skulked like pale fat phantoms in the shadows. In the corner bedroom at the end of the corridor two panes of glass had been blown in.

When I opened the door the gale caught it with great force
and flung it back on its hinges against the wall, and then went
howling down the corridor as though trapped and bursting for
its freedom. There was nothing to be done until the morning,
but I didn't go back downstairs. I sank into a sheeted armchair
and remained there for many hours, such was the lassitude
that overtook me during the long nights, this winter.

There was a lot of death about this winter. A number of my
elderly patients succumbed to cancer though Nan Hale-
Newton hung on grimly. Jean Fig died. She had first been to
see me after that disastrous dinner party, when the mention
of your mother's name had thrown me into such a passion of
misery. In the clear light of day she'd looked even iller. Her
skin still had a distinctly yellowish-green tinge, and the bags
under her eyes were quite as deep and dark as my own.
Jaundice perhaps? After a few polite interchanges I asked her
what appeared to be the problem. "I do hate to bother you,
doctor," she said, "it's probably nothing at all." She'd be a
handsome woman, I remember thinking, if she relaxed a little.
Why was she so tense, so angry—was it Hugh? He'd always
seemed perfectly affable to me. "I'm always tired but I can't
sleep," she said. "And I get these attacks of diarrhea, but I
never know when they're coming." Probably, like most
women of her class, she suffered in a hell of quiet desperation.
"I threw up after dinner and I had to go to the bathroom five
times during the night. I just don't know what's wrong with
me."

"We best take a history then," I said, with some effort
summoning my brisk warm physicianly manner, "and then
I'll examine you."

Jean Fig's history shed no real light on her complaint. The
usual childhood illnesses, a fractured metatarsal at the age of
nineteen when a horse trod on her foot at a gymkhana, married
at twenty-three, no children. "Why no children?" I said.

"We can't," she said. "We've tried, but we can't. I don't know whether it's my fault or Hugh's. He says it's mine, but he never says why he thinks so."

I then asked her to go behind the screens and get undressed. "What, everything?" she said.

Fifteen minutes later she was again sitting across the desk from me. I had probed and prodded and palpated, I had listened to her heart and her lungs, I had tested her reflexes and taken her pulse, which was a bit on the quick side, but apart from this I couldn't find a thing wrong. "Probably a mild attack of gastritis," I said. I made her up a bottle of Mist Explo. "Come back and see me in a couple of weeks, will you?"

"What exactly is gastritis, Dr. Haggard?" she said, taking a few coins out of her purse.

"Not serious," I said, "mild inflammation of the mucous membrane of the stomach. Should settle down pretty quickly."

"And would that make me tired?"

"It might." I screwed the cap on my fountain pen and took off my spectacles and rubbed my eyes. I hadn't slept.

"And look." She lowered her head. "You see? I'm losing my hair."

I frowned. Probably neurotic. Not enough sex, not enough love, too much quiet desperation. She was drying up like a forgotten apple in a neglected bowl. Impossible, I reflected, to fathom the hell that existed behind the facade of an English marriage—hadn't I seen the example of your parents? What vile tortures, I reflected, what unspeakable cruelties were unleashed when the last guest left and the front door closed and like a black and pestilential fog intimacy once more descended! "Let's see what happens when that gastritis clears up," I said. Though I supposed it might be equally possible that when the last guest left and the front door closed ecstasy erupted, sensual joy, active love. Caring, candor, and affection. Unlikely, but possible. I made a note in my desk calendar, and we both rose to our feet. "Good morning, Mrs. Fig."

"Good morning, Dr. Haggard. And thank you."

When I saw her next there was little improvement. Still that worrying yellowish tinge to her skin, and no real change in her inability to keep food down. I examined her again, and again failed to find anything wrong. I felt more sure than ever that the problem was not organic at all, but psychological. Again I delicately broached the subject of her relations with her husband. It was hard for her to be frank with me, but after some gentle prodding she admitted that Hugh had indeed become distant from her, had withdrawn from her, and that they'd lost a connectedness they'd had for years, a connectedness she treasured for it was, she thought, what love is. "I'm sure it's all my fault," she said, "feeling ill all the time, having no energy, losing my hair—what husband wants to come home to a creature like this?" By then the poor woman was in tears. "I'm trying to make an effort," she said, "but it does no good. He acts as though I'm not even there."

And sex?

"Sex?"

The question embarrassed her. She had to be coaxed. But at last I got her to speak. In the past, she told me, they'd made love regularly, three or four times a month, and they'd always shown each other physical affection, hugs and strokes and so on. But all that had stopped, and she thought her own ill health had as much to do with it as Hugh's neglect: she was always so tired she had neither energy nor desire, the only desire she had was for sleep. Even so she had made an effort, she had tried, despite her exhaustion, numerous times to initiate lovemaking, but Hugh wasn't interested. She had assumed he was preoccupied with his work, and she'd tried to get him to talk to her about it, but this had failed to elicit anything either. Probably it was just a phase he was going through. Men were such odd, incomprehensible creatures, she said, and it was so hard to make them *talk*.

"I see."

I was now completely convinced that her anxiety about her marriage was contributing to her ill health, which in turn was affecting her relations with her husband—she was caught in a vicious spiral, the distressed mind producing physical symptoms which then compounded the original problem. I told her all this.

"I'm doing it to myself?" she said, a note of annoyance creeping in here. "I'm making my own hair fall out? I'm turning my own skin yellow?"

"I think you probably are," I said.

For a moment I thought she might tell me to go to hell, but she didn't. Pity. It would probably have done her good. I sold her a bottle of Mist Explo and sent her on her way.

Jean Fig's condition continued to deteriorate and eventually, after consulting her husband, I decided she should be admitted to a private asylum in Bognor Regis. Hugh visited her every weekend, but her condition worsened. I was later told by the superintendent of the asylum that she had for some time before her death refused to see a doctor, claiming that none of us knew what was wrong with her. A tragedy. She was buried in the graveyard in Griffin Head, and I found myself more moved by her funeral than I'd expected to be. Hugh Fig was dignified and manly in his grief.

Was it nephritis, I now wonder? Kidney disease? And I think quite probably it was.

In the meantime of course war had been declared. We were at war. I remember reading the paper at breakfast the morning of September the fourth. Mrs. Gregor said little, as usual, but it was not hard to know what was going through her mind. I like a lightly boiled egg for my breakfast in the autumn and winter months, with half a slice of dry toast and two cups of

tea—like yourself I've always been a light eater. As I read
the paper that Monday I kept an eye on Mrs. Gregor, on the
assumption that what she felt the country felt, for she'd always
seemed to me to be a sort of weather vane in this regard. That
morning there was purpose and vigor in the way she set the
water on the stove to boil—spooned tea into the teapot—
sliced the loaf for toast. She was eager, I could tell, to get
the job started and get it done. No more waiting-and-seeing,
no more hoping for the best. She was ready.

And you? At the time I had no idea that our lives were
moving inexorably closer, though there was perhaps something, that morning, that made me think of your mother with
a more vivid apprehension than usual, she seemed more distinctly *with me*, at the outbreak of war, than she had for some
weeks—was this a premonition of her imminent death? Or
was it, I wonder now, the first dawning glimmer of awareness
I had of your approach?

The old people seemed not to share the general mood, the
grim sense of purpose I detected in Mrs. Gregor. They remembered too well the horrors of '14–'18. The intimation of
personal mortality made the prospect of mass death abhor-
rent—this I could understand: the scale shifts, the private end
becomes insignificant in the epidemic. It seemed to the old
men and women who came into my surgery that morning that
a sickness was upon us, and what galled them most was the
warmth of its welcome; but they had neither the will nor the
strength to resist. Then, as I went through the town on my
rounds that day—and what a beautiful day it was, the weather
was warm and clear and windless for the first days of war—I
saw a gaggle of evacuated London schoolchildren down on
the beach, East End children, dressed in rags, with grubby
faces and grazed knees, screaming with pleasure as they scam-
pered barefoot from the incoming tide—they'd never seen
the sea before. Further along, soldiers were digging up the
beach to fill sandbags. When I got home in the late afternoon

Mrs. Gregor was busy with brown paper, sticky tape and drawing pins, blacking out the windows of the rooms I used at night. It depressed me not to be able to gaze out of the study window, so I took to going up to the top-floor rooms and used them for my nocturnal sea-gazing.

Actually I do know what you were doing at the outbreak of war, for you've told me. Practicing battle climbs to thirty thousand feet, where oxygen hissed into your face mask from a black steel cylinder behind the armored bulkhead. Firing your guns into the sea and raising a jagged plume of foam on the water. Cloud flying and night flying, air drills and battle practice, and getting to know Spitfires—and how you loved Spitfires! You were never able properly to explain to me the joy of flying a Spitfire, but I think perhaps I understand. You told me how you once climbed through twenty-seven thousand feet of cloud, passed out, dived for four miles, and recovered consciousness just in time to pull out of it and climb again—in any other aircraft you'd have bought it, you said. Curtains.

My second winter in Elgin. I continued to sustain my love upon the idea of your mother but it was difficult, those long cold nights, not to grieve for the woman herself. Now I truly haunted Elgin with her memory, it served to keep her spirit alive. Late at night I would hear her voice in the top-floor corner room, and despite the frigid chill that hung in the air, and turned my breath to smoke, I'd be aware, as I came hobbling along the passage, of vague ineffable wisps of her fragrance, and when I opened the door and went in I'd be certain she'd been there. These delicate impressions of her presence enabled me to sustain her, though it was only possible in the long watches of the night, when no other human presence interfered.

During the day I continued to practice medicine, though with no great effectiveness I fear. That winter no bombs fell, though we had certainly been expecting them. We knew what

had happened to Barcelona, buildings flattened, streets filled
with dead and dying, the sky black with enemy aeroplanes—
but no, no bombs fell, and the only war casualties I had to
deal with were caused by the blackout. Hardly a night passed
without someone falling down a flight of steps or walking in
front of a bicycle. One man was brought in with a broken leg
after toppling off the platform at the railway station; fortunately no train was coming. Another broke his nose when he
walked into a tree. Treating these casualties of the blackout
I found it impossible not to think of your mother in a bed in
St. Basil's, with you and Ratcliff standing over her. What was
her last thought? Had it been of me? Had she called out my
name—had your eyes flickered to Ratcliff's—had there been
a frown, a shake of the head—?

Dear James. I sometimes think your coming to Elgin saved
my life. That long, terrible winter after she died was almost
the end of me. I had lost her a second time, I was doubly
bereft, and it was barely possible at times to keep going. The
night I climbed down the cliff, and raged along the beach in
the darkness—that night I'd resolved to keep her flame alive
in my heart, and console myself with poetry and memories,
the husks and shadows of love. But after she died at times
the flame guttered, and I lost faith in the ongoing viability of
her spirit. Then I would storm around Elgin crying my despair,
my fury, my grief, my loss. I would give up medicine, I cried—
I had done my service, I could do no more—*non serviam*, it
was enough. Oh, it was a cold winter, the coldest of my life,
and it should have marked the end of the story. The flame
had burned brightly, then died; all that was left was work and
death. Until you came. Your coming marked an end to that
terrible bleak season—

I knew who you were. The afternoon you appeared in my
surgery, I knew who you were. I'd been reading Goethe,
Faust, I remember—"eternal womanhood leads us above"—
rather prophetic! But yes, I knew who you were, I'd seen you

at her funeral—and oh, the change your coming was to make to my life . . . The story was not over, after all; there was another chapter yet to be written, a final flourish, and why? You, that's why; because you had come. You aroused feelings in me I thought I would never know again. This limping shadow I'd become, with broken hip, broken heart, broken hopes—I seemed now to step into the light of day, to come properly to life once more. Blood coursed in my veins, my heart beat with fresh life, there was zest and vigor in all I did. Mrs. Gregor remarked on the change; she said she'd not seen me looking so well since I'd first come to Elgin. I could tell she approved. She disliked my melancholy, and the irregular habits it encouraged. All that spring you visited me in Elgin, and I awoke happy in the morning, and not even the stretch of bad weather we had in June could dampen my mood. There was rain and fog, clouds and thunderstorms, all of which served to incite Spike to particularly vicious flare-ups, all of which I dealt with as I always have, but even Spike I could now tolerate with benign resignation, with grace.

Whenever I was up at the station I took the opportunity to look for you in the mess or the dispersal hut. The strain on all you fighter boys was palpable now, as you waited for the onslaught that we knew was bound to come. In the past weeks Hitler's armies had swept across Europe smashing everything in their path. Holland and Belgium had crumbled. France fell in a matter of days. Fears of an invasion on the south coast of England began to be voiced with increasing frequency. But first would come the air assault, and what you boys wanted more than anything was to get on with it. Such courage you displayed, such heroism—I felt privileged to witness it, though of course I never said this, for if there was anything you hated it was being what you called "romanticized." But why shouldn't I romanticize you? You were romantic in the original sense of the word. You engaged the enemy in single combat, man to man. You were gallant. You were chivalrous.

You were brave. Why not romantic? You were knights of the
air; and you, dear James, you were *my* knight, my gentle,
parfit knight, you were one of that brave doomed breed sick
with nostalgia for something worth fighting for, something
worth dying for—

But what for me was most remarkable, at the time, was the
sense I had of being liberated at last from grief. My spirits
were rising, and not mine alone; there was a new feeling
abroad, I had detected it in Mrs. Gregor, for there had come,
with the fall of France, and the knowledge that we now stood
alone, a sense of exhilaration combined, curiously, with a
desire, albeit oblique and perverse, for things to get worse,
to get as bad as possible, until we were, as a people, staring
directly into the abyss, so that *then* we might fight back—we
seemed to need to have it confirmed that the situation was
hopeless before the impulse of resistance could be properly
aroused. Oh, they were extraordinary days, and I was no less
affected by the mood of them than anyone else, though my
exhilaration was not provoked just by the threat of invasion,
no, I was exhilarated for different reasons, for reasons of my
own. For this was the period when you were visiting me
regularly in Elgin.

And then—disaster. James, did I have to lose you as well—
was it inevitable? I'd already had my forebodings, and sown
my seed of unease, for I was desperate to keep you coming
back; but I had not been wise. You did come back, but on
your face an expression I'd never seen before, a sulky, boyish
resentment touched with real anger. You'd stood at the front
door of Elgin taut and coiled like a spring, and I brought you
straight into the surgery. "Drink?"

"No thank you. I came to talk to you about what you said
about my mother."

"Oh?" Frowning, my eyes averted, I busied myself with
cigarettes.

"Yes. You suggested she wasn't treated properly."

"Did I say that?"

"That was the impression you gave me."

"I certainly didn't intend to."

"Then why did you say you wished you could have seen her?"

"Not because I felt she was being treated incompetently."

"Then why?"

"Why do you think?"

You stared at me furiously, and I was reminded—dreadful memory!—of your father's expression when he attacked me in St. Basil's. "You said kidney conditions were tricky to diagnose."

"So they are."

"So why would you say that unless to suggest she was being treated incompetently?"

"Do you think she was being treated incompetently?"

"I?" This caught you off guard.

"Yes you. Weren't you concerned?"

"If I was concerned I spoke to my father."

"And?"

"He told me everything was being done that could be done."

"But you weren't sure."

"Why shouldn't I be sure?"

I shrugged. "You're so angry about it now."

"Don't you think my father would have known if there was any way to treat her?"

"You've spoken to him again?"

"Yes I have."

"And what did he say about me?"

"He said—"

"What?"

"You were not her attending physician. How could you know?"

"I expect he said more than that. I expect he told you I

was unreliable and untrustworthy and that you should have
nothing to do with me."

You glared at me and said nothing.

"All the same you've come back to tell me this. Why?
Because you suspect there's something in what I say. You're
not convinced your father's telling you the truth."

This was going too far. Face ablaze you rose abruptly to
your feet and left the room. Damn! Damn damn damn! I had
misjudged you—misjudged how much in thrall you were to
Ratcliff. A moment later the front door banged behind you.
I sat there smoking until forced by his clamoring to attend to
Spike.

Then three days later I heard the news that I suppose unconsciously I'd been dreading all spring: you'd been injured.
I was in the surgery seeing to Spike when the call came
through. It was the adjutant from the station. "B Flight?" I
cried—that was your flight—"Who?"

It was you.

Five minutes later I was in the car and turning out onto the
coast road. The alarm I'd felt on hearing that it was you—the
vehemence of it surprised me. In my imagination I saw your
Spitfire cartwheeling across the airfield, smashing itself to
pieces and you lying in the wreckage broken and dying. Then
the adjutant told me there'd been heavy flak over Dover and
you'd caught some of it chasing a Dornier down. "Badly hit?"
I said.

"He got out of his kite by himself," he said, "but he's not
happy."

The station sick bay was another of those single-story prefabricated buildings clustered in the shadow of a hangar. The
main room had half a dozen beds, three down each side; off
it was a side room where the medical officer worked, and it
was there that I found you. You were standing at the window,
and as I came hurrying in I noted the ragged rip in your

trousers, just below the waist but well to the right of the spine. Blood had stained the fabric around the wound. "James," I cried, "you've been hit!"

You turned stiffly toward me, wincing, clearly in some pain. Your face was set in hard and hostile lines. "Stung a bit," you said curtly.

"Let's have a look at it then."

The great worry with such penetrating injuries is the spinal cord, the risk of damage to the vertebrae. Your tunic came off easily enough, and your trousers, but your shirt and underpants were stuck to the wound with dried blood and I had to pull the fabric smartly from the flesh, which made you wince. I sat in a chair and you stood with your back to me, in the light, while I examined the wound. It was narrow, ragged, and deep; it seemed probable that a small piece of shrapnel had embedded itself in the muscle of your upper buttock but without affecting backbone or fatty tissue, so there was no immediate danger of infection. I would need to get an X-ray to confirm it, of course, but I didn't think we had to worry about tetanus. I told you all this. There was an examination table on the far side of the room. "Lie down flat," I said, "and I'll clean you up. Have to give you a shot of something, I'm afraid."

"Do your worst," you murmured, climbing gingerly onto the table as I prepared the syringe. I injected into the muscle close to the wound; I noticed as I did so that the texture of your skin was like your mother's, there was the same silky feeling when I touched you. I paused a moment to let the anesthetic take effect—and to my great annoyance, unexpected and unwanted, grief arose, and I had to turn away, hold myself rigid as the wave passed through me. After a moment I was under control and I forced myself to concentrate on the work at hand. Then I was stitching the wound, and James, were I stitching the face of a beautiful woman I don't think I'd have taken more pains about it. I closed it all coarsely with catgut, then sewed the superficial skin with silkworm gut and completed the job with stitching so fine your flesh would carry no scar. It was fastidious, time-consuming work, but had it been your mother on the table I would have made every effort; I could do no less for you. I doubt your father could have done as elegant a piece of stitching.

Eventually it was finished, and you climbed down. I was washing my hands. "No more flying for you for a while," I said, glancing at your reflection in the mirror over the sink. You were shuffling across the room, the neat cluster of stitches stark against the white flesh of your upper buttock. You reached for the dressing gown hanging on a hook on the door, and for just a second, as you pulled it on, I caught a glimpse, in my mirror, of the front of your body. Frowning, I turned round, picked up a towel and dried my hands. I was puzzled at what I'd seen. There appeared to be something rather peculiar about your penis.

That night in Elgin I thought again about what I'd seen, and I was concerned. As a doctor, I was concerned. As a man, however, as a *friend*—I was wounded by the coldness and hostility you'd displayed. Though I could at least console myself that you'd have to see me once more, if only to have your stitches out. When that happened I would treat you, I decided, with brisk neutral professional courtesy. You could make the first approach to reconciliation, as and when it suited you. *If* it suited you—

I was in the surgery when you came into my waiting room a few days later. I had your X-rays on the desk in front of me. There was, indeed, as I'd suspected, a fragment of metal lodged in muscle in your lower back, but there was no point in trying to dig it out as it posed no risk of infection. I brought you into the surgery and asked you to get undressed; I was still curious about what had seemed, in the brief glimpse I'd had of you in the sick bay, to be some slight genital abnormality.

You emerged from behind the screen, and I watched you closely as you moved across the surgery. I had you stand in the middle of the room. What I saw, as I rose from my desk, was a small, pale, perfectly made young man with black hair, narrow shoulders, slim hips, and an almost complete absence of body hair. There was a tendency to infantilism of the sexual organs; there was also a slight convergence of the lower limbs toward the knees, and imperceptible, perhaps, to any but the trained medical eye, mild gynecomastia with slight enlargement of the nipple. It instantly suggested nascent glandular disturbance, which was worrying. I approached, frowning, pulled over a chair and examined you more closely. Your skin, I again noted, was oddly smooth to my fingers. I paid particular attention to the penis, plump and soft like a child's, and the testes, cupping them in my hand, weighing them. Froehlich's syndrome, perhaps? They were rather small. You grew suddenly impatient. "That's enough of that," you said. I rose to my feet, and you stepped swiftly over to the examination table and lay down flat on your stomach. At the time I had no real knowledge of the pathology, though I was aware that shock, or violent emotional upset, could produce disorders of the endocrine system. "Had any bad shocks lately?" I murmured as I started taking out your stitches.

Muffled snort from you. "Plenty of shocks in this war."

"Ah."

You were dressed again and sitting across from me on the other side of the desk. Tricky things, endocrine disorders, and I wasn't certain just what would happen next. My concern was that it might get out of hand, and I thought you should see a specialist. But when I mentioned this you very curtly ruled it out, the mere suggestion of a visit to London. You told me, with some impatience, that the squadron was way

below full strength; the new pilots had barely had more than
a few hours' experience in Spitfires, and needed constant help
and surveillance; and anyway, you said, there was little to
defend these shores but the few fighter squadrons that remained operational. This was no time to disappear up to London to see specialists, you said, and anyway why? You felt
fine. There was nothing wrong with you, beyond a bit of
shrapnel in your back. Your duty lay here in Griffin Head, on
this point you were adamant.

I understood of course your need to deny what must have
been extremely disturbing to you, these curious changes occurring in your body. I began to tell you about the pituitary
gland and its secretion of estrogen: if your pituitary was mal-
functioning there should be no delay in seeking specialized
help. But you wouldn't hear of it, you angrily cut me off before
I'd properly made my point. Not until it was over, you said.
"What, the war?" I cried.

"No," you said, "the Battle of Britain."

The Battle of Britain. It was the first time I'd heard the
phrase. Now that the Battle of France was over, the Battle of
Britain would begin. It would be fought in the air, for in order
to invade England Hitler must get his army across the Channel
unmolested by the RAF; he must wipe out the RAF first. So
I shouldn't have been surprised that you chose to stand and
fight. You were putting your country first.

The next days were not easy for me. I had been sleeping
badly, so I was tired, which made Spike vicious, which in
turn interfered with my rest. I spent much time pacing my
study through the long watches of the night, from time to
time going down the path at the back of Elgin to stand on
the cliffs and watch the searchlights. You were constantly on
my mind. I pictured the dispersal hut: little more than a shed
really, with a stove in the middle and a pipe going out through
the roof, a few old armchairs and couches scrounged from

various barns, a table with a telephone on it and a few charts
and notices tacked to the walls. On warm days you'd drag the
chairs outside onto the grass at the edge of the airfield,
otherwise you'd be clustered round the stove with your feet
up reading newspapers or novels or playing chess, ready to go
when the phone rang and the word came through to scramble.
How was it for you? Those others, they had only Messerschmitts to worry about, the threat they faced was clearly
defined. Their enemy came from across the Channel, from
Germany. Not yours; you had an enemy within you, but what
was it, exactly? Was it Froehlich's, as I suspected? Your fat
distribution was certainly feminoidal, but it lacked the marked
deposit on lower belly and thighs that one associates with
Froehlich's. Perhaps, I hazarded, the constant anxiety of warfare, as experienced by the fighter pilot, could cause endocrine
disturbances of such severity as to effect visible changes in
the body's sexual characteristics—?

Several days passed, and you did not come to see me. I looked
for you whenever I was up at the station, but for some reason
you were never around. Then one afternoon, just as I was
leaving the sick bay, I saw a Spitfire coming in to land that I
recognized as yours, and after it had taxied to a stop I limped
across the grass to meet you. You heaved out your parachute
and jumped down off the wing. You seemed distinctly dis-
pleased to see me; you gave me a brief nod then turned your
back on me. "James," I said, in as pleasant and reasonable a
tone as I could muster, "why don't you come down to the
surgery tomorrow. I'd like to have another look at you."

You ignored me. You began talking to your fitter about your
guns. I persisted; wasn't your welfare my responsibility now?
"I've dug up some gen that might interest you," I said.

"I'm on ops tomorrow," you said, your back still to me.

"Can't let it go too long," I said.

At last you turned to me. You flung off your flying helmet
and began angrily wiping your hands on an oily rag. "Look

doctor," you said—and your eyes were flashing with anger!—
"why don't we just forget all about it? I'm all right, do you
understand?"

"Up to you," I said. "But I can't believe this isn't preying
on your mind. Talking it over might help."

"It certainly would not help," you snapped. "Now please
excuse me, I have an aeroplane to see to."

"But James," I cried, "you're sick!"

You turned to me. "Not me, doctor," you said shortly.
"You."

That was all we said. I was unwilling to put pressure on
you; I thought it quite possible that the best thing for you
might be just to get on with your war and not pay undue
attention to what was, after all, not a life-threatening condition. But I did notice that it was progressing, I could tell by
your skin, your voice, your general demeanor. Impossible of
course to know what was happening elsewhere to the body,
I'd need to examine you for that, and there seemed little
likelihood, the frame of mind you were in, of your permitting
that. But I could imagine how alarming it was, seeing your
body behave so oddly, and in all probability having to deal
with urges and desires that issued from what must have felt
like an alien creature within you.

Meanwhile it was becoming clearer to all that command of
the air was the necessary precondition for invasion. The Luft-
waffe was attacking the RAF by day and by night, in the air
and on the ground. Only when the RAF was knocked out
could a landing in England be undertaken. Churchill said that
the future of civilization depended on you. If you failed, he
said—that is, if the RAF failed to repel the German air assault,
which would open the way to a landing on the south coast—
the world would sink into the abyss of a new dark age made
sinister by the light of perverted science.

This then was the end of the brief idyllic phase of our friendship. I saw much less of you after the Battle of Britain began;

you were on two-minute alert from dawn to dusk, and had little desire to spend your evenings in Elgin. I can understand why. You were in a state of physical and emotional exhaustion, and cared for little but sleep, and the company of other fighter pilots, for they alone shared what you were going through. Not everything. Only I was aware of your medical predicament, the mutiny of your disturbed and raging glands. Late at night I pored over books in the upstairs back bedroom and thought about you, puzzled over what it meant, that you seemed to be growing paler, softer, quieter by the day. Eventually it became clear to me that I had stumbled upon a pathological phenomenon previously unknown to medical science. The effect on the endocrine system of acute, sustained emotional pressure had never been properly studied, presumably because the conditions necessary to provoke it—intense, high-speed air combat for instance—had never existed before. I suspected that fear—specifically, the constant terror of sudden violent death—could produce, in individuals of a certain predisposition, disturbances of the pituitary gland that could cause changes in the body related to the secretion of hormones. It was a new syndrome, perhaps even a new disease, a disease unique to modern warfare. But I could only write it up if you'd allow me to examine you, take a history, attempt treatment—and this, clearly, you were not prepared to do. Perhaps if you would ever let me examine you again I could do a proper case study and write a monograph. Publish an account of the diagnosis and treatment of the disease. *Name* it, even—*Haggard's disease?* But no; ignoble thought; I pushed it out of my mind. You were suffering, that was all, and it was my duty to relieve that suffering.

In August the weather improved. It was clear, still and warm, a lovely English summer, but these were the worst conditions for an overworked, undermanned air force whose pilots were close to exhaustion. Every day you went up five, six, seven

times. The sky over Griffin Head was crisscrossed with con-
trails that unraveled like rolled bandages as Spitfires fought
Messerschmitts escorting bombers whose targets were the air-
fields of southern England. Casualties were heavy. The station
was attacked again and I was there. It was one of those warm,
cloudless days, utterly tranquil—until, that is, the message
came over the loudspeaker: "Large enemy bombing formation
approaching Griffin Head. All personnel not engaged in active
duty take cover immediately." I looked up but I couldn't see
or hear a thing in that clear blue summer sky. All round the
field men were running for shelter. A Spitfire came past me
with a roar to take off downwind and it was then that I saw
them, a dozen black shapes shining in the sun and coming
straight on. I stood transfixed, fascinated, mesmerized—this
was the enemy.

Then came the rising scream of the first bomb—I came to
my senses—and threw myself onto the grass, covering my
head. Through my fingers I watched the Spitfire take off, and
it occurred to me that you might be flying it. It was about
twenty feet off the ground when suddenly it catapulted upward as though on a piece of elastic, came down on its back
and plowed along the runway upside down. The next moment
a load of dirt hit me and then I heard someone shouting,
"Run, for Christ's sake!" I peered round, spitting dirt out of
my mouth, and saw the adjutant standing in the door of a
shelter and waving wildly at me. Somehow I got myself over
there. My first thought was of my black bag, somewhere out
on the field; my second was of you, and whether you were in
the crashed Spitfire. I started to ask where you were, but the
scream and crump of falling bombs made it impossible to be
heard. The air was thick with dust and the shelter heaved
with each explosion, and for several minutes I believed that
you were dead, and that I would shortly be dead also. Then
the bombing stopped. There was a moment of utter silence
in the shelter before we emerged into the fresh air.

The runway was torn apart. It was full of gaping holes. There were mounds of earth everywhere. A lorry lay on its side by the dispersal hut, one wheel torn off. Smoke drifted in the still, silent air. The Spitfire had come to a halt halfway down the runway, where it lay upside down but not burning. An ambulance was racing across the grass toward it. "Whose aeroplane?" I cried.

"Johnny Hart, poor sod," someone said.

"Right," I said. Not yours! Then I saw my bag, apparently undamaged, sitting on top of a large gobbet of dirt. Off I limped, with Spike screaming like the blazes in my hip. There was nothing I could do for Johnny Hart. He hung limp in his harness, upside down with a broken neck. All I could think was, it might have been you. It might have been you. Then: it would be you. One day, it would be you. Not perhaps upside down with a broken neck, but plunging in flames into the Channel, going out in a blaze of glory . . . The life expectancy of fighter pilots in the Battle of Britain was not long.

By night I watched searchlights slicing across the darkness, and heard the bark of the ack-ack guns. Sometimes I'd walk down through the back garden to the edge of the cliff, and in the warm night air gaze out across the Channel toward the French coast, and sense there the waiting evil. I feared for you. I telephoned the station every evening and discreetly inquired after you. I came up at every opportunity, and it was a mark of the stress you were all under that your banter grew rougher as your stamina declined. I didn't mind, of course I didn't, I understood the pressure you were under. You'd be lounging about in battered armchairs, maps stuffed down your flying boots, uniforms creased and baggy, no collar and tie of course, just a piece of silk tied round your neck. You were the long-haired fighter boys, scruffy, cynical and brave, England's last hope. And you, dear boy, you lounged there too, as though to the manner born, you were fighting and surviving with the best of them, and only I knew how sick you were.

• • •

No, you never came to see me in Elgin anymore. At first I didn't mind, for I knew what you were up against, all of you. Then I faced up to the fact that there was more to it than this, and that you were deliberately avoiding me. What made it worse was your unfriendliness up at the station. You were aware, whenever I came into the mess, or the dispersal hut, that my eyes would always seek you first, but you no longer met my gaze. You turned away as though I were a stranger. On one occasion you slid down into your armchair, stretched your legs out, tipped your cap forward over your eyes and pretended to be asleep. You barely troubled to conceal a yawn. Later, when I thought about it, I realized why you were acting this way: you were angry with me because I *knew*. You had suddenly shied away, withdrawn from me, because you couldn't admit to this physical embarrassment that must every day be growing more pronounced, more inescapable.

This was painful to contemplate. It was obvious to me how desperately you must need not only treatment but a sensitive ear, how you must be craving affection and understanding. Who else could you turn to? Certainly not Ratcliff. But I could have been of real help to you, for I had an idea of what you were going through, and could grasp the horror of it all. I look at what nature has given me—I am not a tall man, in fact my body is barely bigger than a child's, and yet I have a man's head, full-sized, with a great shock of hair that spills from my brow in the manner of the late Beethoven and does nothing but emphasize the ill-proportion of my anatomy. Since Spike my gait is wretched, I shuffle and limp, I have gray skin, and this curiously vivid streak of white in my hair that springs up off my forehead like a fountain of ice. When I think that this botched and crippled structure is the frame for the spirit that burns within it, burns with a passion and at times a grandeur that few men know—it's a joke, a travesty, and as a result I have learned to cultivate impotence, of a sort, as a way of life.

But you! You were still a young man—and I remembered what it was to be young, to be fit and strong, to live in a young man's body. When a young man's body is functioning properly there is no better place on earth than inside it.

Oh, but I missed your friendship too—was it wrong to think of myself? I was no stranger to loss and loneliness, God knows I drank deep enough of both in the wake of your mother's rejection. To lose you, however, so soon after finding you— I was quite desperately disheartened by this. I remember stopping at the Elms and going in to see Nan Hale-Newton. She was still hanging on; though riddled with cancer she wasn't letting go, she hadn't finished with the injections, as she told her perplexed daughter Marjorie. It always did me good to see her, I admired the ferocity of her determination not to surrender to the darkness until she chose to do so. "In my own good time, Haggard," she would tell me, "that's when I'll be going out." Marjorie was a good and devoted nurse, and as a result was turning into a spinster, but if Nan felt any guilt at being the instrument of her daughter's progressive desiccation she never expressed it. "That girl's getting to be an old maid," she'd sniff, after Marjorie had left the sickroom and I was preparing the needle.

"It's your fault," I'd say (we spoke candidly, she wouldn't tolerate any other sort of conversation).

"Nonsense. Marjorie's got a mind of her own. Let her go out and live her life. Nobody's stopping her."

"No, nobody's *stopping* her."

"No one has to do what they don't want to."

"So what would happen to you?"

"Me?" A muffled hoot. "What does it matter about me? An old bag with one foot in the grave, what do I matter?" She refused to acknowledge Marjorie's predicament.

So I turned into the Elms late one afternoon after visiting the station and being cruelly reminded yet again that you had spurned me. Marjorie took me up and left me with her mother.

"So what's the matter with you?" The voice had turned into a dry, hoarse rasp but it had lost none of its authority. The curtains were drawn, the room was full of shadows, and also of that awful pervasive smell of a failing, diseased body, inactive too long; broken vessel of a still-vigorous flame. Her eyes glinted in the sunken skull, a few dry gray wisps of hair framing it like a halo. "What's on your mind, Haggard, spit it out. No, let me guess. It's that young pilot of yours."

I'd told her about you. Not everything, but who you were, who your mother was.

"Has he been shot down?" she said. "I hear them up there, killing each other."

I said you had no time for me anymore.

"Not surprised! Why would he pay any attention to an old cripple like you?"

For some reason, I don't know why, fatigue perhaps, this was too much. I was unable to suppress a sob. "Oh for God's sake man," said Nan Hale-Newton. "Come on, where's my injection? Here I am suffering the torments of the damned and you're blubbing like a gel."

She was right of course. I opened my black bag. A little later she was breathing gently and her eyes were closed. Spike was being a bloody nuisance so I broke open another ampoule and relieved my own pain. I sat there by her bed, my breathing in unison with hers, my face softened by the same sad smile, until after half an hour or so Marjorie came up to see if there was anything wrong.

A curious thing happened on my way out of the Elms. I came downstairs with Marjorie and saw standing on the hall floor a large cardboard box full of Nan's clothes. Marjorie noticed me staring at it and said: "They're for the evacuees. I don't suppose you're going past the church, doctor?"

"What?" I was transfixed—there was a fur coat in that heap of discarded garments *exactly the same color as your mother's.*

Marjorie repeated her request. "Yes," I murmured, "yes of course I will."

"Somebody should have the use of them," she said. "Mummy won't wear them again."

I dropped off Marjorie's box of clothes at the church, but not before I'd taken out the fur coat. That would go home with me to Elgin.

Often I stood at the edge of the airfield and watched you land. I'd see the cockpit hood pushed back as you brought the aeroplane down, I'd see you glance out, your goggles pushed up on top of your flyer's helmet and the strip of silk at your throat fluttering wildly in the wind. What a beautiful machine it was, with its trim deceptive frailty, its wickedly simple lines! The ground crew would be waiting, the fire tender, the ambulance. You'd cut the engine and the Spitfire would seem almost to float down, then you'd lift the nose just a hair, bump down on all three wheels, and let the aeroplane run off its speed. You'd disconnect the radio and oxygen leads, release your safety straps, then swing your legs up and over onto the wing—and that's how I'll remember you, squinting at the sun from the wing of a Spitfire, and only I aware of the bizarre physical transformation you were undergoing. Though if you saw me you'd walk off in the opposite direction.

Why so cruel? Was it only because I knew about your condition? Perhaps there was more to it than this. Perhaps it was because you were your mother's son. It daily became clearer to me that I had to do something. You were suffering exquisite misery, and only I could relieve your pain. It was my duty. Oh, but these were hard times and I began to feel terribly dispirited. I began to feel I would never know anything but loss. There was one night that I reached for your mother in the darkness—in my mind, I mean, for it had become a habit over time to feel for her presence in memory and feeling, if not in physical reality, when I was alone and melancholy late at night—and she wasn't there! She wasn't there! I could summon the image of the woman but it was a bare, stark memory, no more, it was bereft of emotion—I felt nothing!

I had never known this before. To fail to feel—this truly was loss, and I was bewildered, frightened, dismayed. I'd been in the upstairs corner room among the sheeted armchairs, watching the moon on the sea; the black fur coat was draped about my shoulders, it reminded me of her, it helped me identify myself with her living spirit—until now! I left the room in high panic and came down the stairs in a very frenzy of alarm, down through the darkened house. Into the study, and a frantic groping in the drawer of my desk—not there! Down the next flight, good leg bad leg stick, across the hall and into the surgery, and just as I thought, I found it in the drawer—the fly-in-glass. I stood in the darkened surgery and clutched it tight, and as I'd hoped and prayed it would it began to generate comfort, in the form, faint at first, but slowly gaining power, of pain. The old pain, pain the familiar. The ache, the bite of the pain—it was Spike remembering, not I, it was Spike who held her memory and all the associated emotion—Spike it was who held the slim phantom close, held her clinging to the pin in my hip like a plasmid substance, translucent, faintly shining, trembling to life now in the darkness, and I sank into my chair and reached for my black bag, relieved that the crisis was past. The idea came to me then that memory was less a faculty of the mind than of the body, for with the easing of Spike's pain so did the memory of your mother cease to harrow me with hopeless longing.

And then I had the most peculiar and vivid sensation: I felt her presence. Not as I'd felt it before, when by dint of sustained reverie I'd aroused a wisp of her perfume, the sound of her voice—at those times there seemed only the most delicate membrane separating the construct of aroused memory from her actual presence, only the thinnest of veils—no, it was not the willed evocation of her, which invariably brought

in its wake tears of frustration as I railed against my inability
to break through and make of the phantom a woman—it was
not that, it was a tranquil, unstrained conviction that an-
nounced itself calmly and that filled me with the sure knowledge that she was, yes, viable still in the world, and inhabited
the body of her son: she had come back to me.

I rose from my chair and pulling the fur snugly about me
I climbed the stairs to the top of the house, where I could
gaze at the sea and attempt to assimilate the idea. The profound physical likeness of mother and son, and your emergent
womanhood—I had been quite wrong to think exclusively in
terms of glandular disease. Explanation—*pathos* and *logos*—
could not begin to encompass what was happening to you,
the miraculous change that was even now being effected by
the movement of her spirit into your body.

A long night, as I pondered all this, but eventually for a
few short hours I slept. When I awoke, the whole tissue of
thought and wonder collapsed. It all seemed the most pre-
posterous nonsense. The doctor within me spoke, he scoffed
with skepticism—movement of spirit in the world? A fevered
imagination, erotic obsession exacerbated by morphia—the
boy was victim of glandular disease and suffering agonies of
confusion as a result—this was my concern, my sole concern.
So said the doctor. And so did he believe, as he went about
his duties that day.

But come nightfall I was no longer sure. Watching the
searchlights sweeping across a black sky, feeling the pressure
of ideas that owed little to the cautious half-truths of empi-
ricism, I was convinced again that the soul of a dead woman
cried out to her lover through the body of her son. I stood in
front of the window, wearing the fur, and saw her gazing back
at me; and I knew I was right. It was many hours until I slept;
and when at last I did slip away I dreamed a very curious
dream.

•   •   •

There was a Heinkel in trouble in the sky over Griffin Head. It was one of a group that had crossed the Channel with an escort of Messerschmitts. The squadron scrambled and attacked from the rear, from above, out of the sun; the German fighters took evasive action, going into half-rolls and vertical dives with the Spitfires in hot pursuit. I heard the crackle of machine-gun fire and stopped the car (I was up on the Downs for some reason) to get out and gaze at the sky inland to the north, but all I could see were trails of vapor. The Heinkels, separated from their escort, turned for home and in close formation made for the coast at twelve thousand feet. Somebody on his way back to the airfield—was it you?—spotted them from above and dived straight down in a quarter head-on attack. You got the slowest of them in your sights and let go with all eight guns in several short bursts. Smoke poured from the port engine and the bomber began to lose altitude. At about eight thousand feet it jettisoned its bombs. To no avail; it crashed into the sea and went down in seconds. None of the crew got out. A stick of bombs fell on the outskirts of the town, and several houses sustained extensive damage. One of them was Elgin.

There is a way the body has of postponing pain, of going into shock in the immediate aftermath of trauma. The mind will function in a similar fashion when it must protect itself from too fierce an assault of feeling. This, in the dream, seems to be what happened now: my initial reaction was one of bemusement. Two hours earlier I had left a house. I returned to a smoking ruin. At first I didn't perceive how severe the damage was. There was an eerie silence and the air had a sort of sharp and tremulous clarity. I stood in the driveway, leaning on the door of the Humber, and gazed at the facade of the house, which seemed almost intact—the windows had been blown out, and the roof badly hit, but an initial impression of solidity was there. But slowly my eye moved upward and settled on the strange skeletal pattern of charred rafters arching against the blue afternoon sky like the bones of some prehistoric creature. Several were still burning. Everything was so still! But even as I stood there a clutch of slates went suddenly slithering down and clattered into the wreckage within with a sound like clanging steel. I became aware of the myriad noises of Elgin settling and dying, heaves and groans that were almost human, splinterings and smashes as stresses and pressures were redistributed, realigned. It then occurred to me that the real destruction must be at the back, so I limped round the side of the house, through that oddly trembling, pristine air, picking my way over shattered glass and slates and masonry.

And this was where the bomb had hit. It was as though a huge bite had been taken out of the back of the house. The back porch, the back kitchen, the scullery, the kitchen itself— the rooms above—utterly destroyed. The blast had knocked the walls out sideways. Small fires burned here and there. Strange thing, the way the unconscious mind works, for I perceived not wreckage but fragments of order. Splintered stretches of flooring sagged drunkenly against stumps of walls but here was a table, rubble all round it, and a cup and saucer intact on top. Here was a bundle of newspapers neatly tied with string. Here was the kitchen stove and on it a pot with a wooden spoon, though the pot was full of broken slate. The floors above had fallen in and I came upon part of the wall of my study, and hanging in the middle a painting, undamaged, of a wanderer above a sea of mist. I gingerly picked my way through, my black bag in my hand, still incredulous, as though I were on my way, as usual, to the front of the house for afternoon surgery. And then I saw Mrs. Gregor's shoe.

Spike began to shriek in my hip and I had to sit down. I sat on a kitchen chair amid the rubble and the small fires and opened my black bag. I dissolved a tablet in a teaspoon over a match and managed without mishap to fill a syringe, though my hands were less than steady. A few moments later, com-

posed, somewhat, I leaned over and picked up the shoe. The
tears came. Smoke drifted in thin gray coils into the clear air.
A woman's shoe speaks volumes. Mrs. Gregor's was a stout
brown sensible shoe, well worn; it was still laced up. It was
broad in the instep, for she had a wide foot. Once I held your
mother's shoe, some long-ago afternoon in Jubilee Road. Your
mother's foot was slender and small, she had a delicate foot.
She had a delicate ankle. I remembered kneeling on the rug
in front of the gas fire, with her curled up in the armchair,
after we had made love, and discovering such perfection, such
beauty, in her foot and ankle. At some point I heard the
squadron overhead. During the last weeks, whenever I heard
Spitfires passing over the house, even if I was seeing a patient
I excused myself, and limped off down the passage into the
kitchen, and out through the back door, and lifted my eyes.
Now again I heard the squadron, and I marveled that one
among you carried within his slender androgynous frame a
spirit of courage, and innocence, and youth, and beauty, and
hope. Then I lifted my eyes; sitting on a kitchen chair in the
ruins of Elgin, clutching a dead woman's shoe, I lifted my
eyes to Heaven and dreamed I saw an angel.

An angel—what did *this* mean? What was happening to me—
was I going out of my mind? Was I being driven mad by loss
and starting to confuse reality with the products of my own
grief-torqued imagination? That I could even picture you, poor
sick boy, an angel—and an angel you had certainly appeared,
hairless, translucent, with tiny breasts and a boy's genitalia,
evanescent in the daytime sky and soaring upward like a diver
returning to the surface, and *radiant*—your whole figure *suffused* with light—I sat up violently in bed, Spike awoke with
me, and I stared, unseeing, horrified, hands clasped to my
face, at the back of the bedroom door. What was happening
to me? I arose in haste, shaved hurriedly and made my way
downstairs to the kitchen; Mrs. Gregor was at the stove melt-

ing a lump of lard in the frying pan. The sight of her gave
me comfort. I sank into a chair and groped in my pockets for
a cigarette. "Egg, doctor?" she murmured.

There was a newspaper on the table, and a pot of tea. "Fine,
Mrs. Gregor," I said as I stared unseeing at the war news.

"Sausage, doctor?"

"I beg your pardon?"

"Sausage? Shall I do you a sausage?" She had turned from
the stove and was holding up a large pink pork sausage. The
idea of food was intolerable. I rose unsteadily, left the kitchen,
and hobbled down to the surgery. The morning was quiet; I
had no patients to see, thankfully. At about noon, somewhat
recovered, I heard Mrs. Gregor wheeling her bicycle round
to the front of the house, and from some stray impulse I came
out into the hall to the front door, whence, unobserved, I
watched her lift herself onto the saddle and pedal off down
the drive. The sight gave me pleasure, inasmuch as I was
capable of pleasure, I don't know why; oh, I suppose the
residue of what I'd felt in that dream, on finding her shoe in
the ruins of Elgin—I was relieved that that good woman had
not died after all, and more to the point, still cared enough
about my welfare to appear daily in Elgin.

Later I drove to the Elms to see Nan Hale-Newton. I told
her about my dream. She'd never been bombed, she said,
but she'd lost houses, knew how painful it could be. But only
bricks and mortar, after all, this was her line. Not Elgin, I
said, that house wasn't just bricks and mortar. Nonsense, she
snorted. Then she said an astonishing thing: "You should
marry the woman."

"What woman?"

"Your housekeeper."

"Mrs. Gregor? *Marry* her?" I was bewildered. How on earth
had she jumped to this conclusion?

"Oh, look at yourself, man. You're ill. You're coming apart
at the seams. You never eat. Forever mooning about that damn
boy. Marry the woman, you need someone to look after you.

She'll have you, but not for much longer. Marry her while you still can." Then she sighed. The room was full of shadows. "I'm tired," she said, "I dream about water." I said I didn't know what that meant. We sat there in silence.

I hesitate to tell you what occurred that night. Drawn, irresistibly, to be near you, I drove up to the station. Being now unofficially attached to the medical officer's staff I was admitted by the sentry and parked the car by the sick bay. I knew where the pilots' quarters were; what I hoped to do there I cannot now imagine, simply I was drawn to you like a moth to a flame. Oh, the idea of it now, I shudder at it—I see myself skulking in the shadows of the big silent hangar—there was a moon that night, and little cloud, which made concealment difficult. I see myself darting past the Spitfires in the gloom of the hangar, tiny limping figure in a black fur coat scuttling across a vast space of shadows and aeroplanes. Down the side of the hangar and across to your quarters, another of those prefabricated structures with its corrugated tin roof gleaming dully in the moonlight. I paused, panting, in the shadows. Somewhere within, I knew, you slept. What did I intend to do now? Come to you in the darkness? Hardly! It was mad, mad! But I did not go back, not immediately. I sat on the grass, in the shadows, with my back against the wall, feeling connected with you through mere contact with the building in which you slept.

I returned to Elgin in the early hours of the morning, and went to the surgery and took out your X-rays. For a long time, I don't know how long, I gazed at those shadows, those dim visual echoes of your physical being, and lodged within, the clear hard outline of your shrapnel, your Spike, our material linkage.

The following afternoon I drove up to the station as usual. I parked by the airfield and sat in the car smoking cigarettes. I saw several scrambles before the adjutant came over and asked if he could help me with anything. Nothing, I said. He then told me, with some tact, that my presence was making the pilots uneasy. "You know how superstitious they are," he said. "Would you mind, doctor?" I left the station. I knew where you'd be later: there was a squadron party in the mess.

It was a mild warm evening. Searchlights scissored the darkness, and the night was alive with the boom and clatter of big guns. I walked on the beach, I stumped up and down in my fur, raging in my distraught mind against the prospect of the darkness to come, as the sea hissed and murmured on the Griffin sands, and when, exhausted, and in severe pain, I came into the mess I found that the party was already raucous; the pilots were celebrating. But in all the hilarity there was now a barely concealed tone of fatigue, of desperation, of hysteria even. Five, six, seven times a day you went up. You were losing pilots hourly. The onslaught was relentless. It didn't let up. Wave after wave of them, Dorniers, Heinkels, with their escorts of Messerschmitts—I had seen them, those black aeroplanes shining in the sun, crosses on their wings, droning steadily onward, and committed to our destruction— they were the very manifestation of evil! Of course there was frenzy in your carousing, it was the song of death you roared round the piano.

I approached. You watched me coming toward you. I daresay I seemed absurd to you, I certainly seemed absurd to myself—a tragic figure on a tiny scale, this was me, suffering the agonies of the damned but for what, exactly? "Hello doctor," you said wearily, and turned toward the bar.

"Hello James." My angel! I stood beside you and waited to be served. I offered you a drink but you refused. I ordered a gin. There were loud voices, shouts of laughter, a scrum of large bodies in blue uniforms, but we seemed curiously insulated from it all, you and I. "James," I said, as I busied myself lighting a cigarette, and keeping my eyes averted from you, "have I hurt your feelings?"

The cigarette was lit. I exhaled smoke, took a sip of my gin and only then glanced at you. You were gazing at the rows of bottles behind the bar, and I didn't know what to make of your expression. You lifted your glass to your lips. "You know, I'm only concerned for your well-being. If I've been tactless, in some way—"

Your eyebrows lifted a fraction.

"If I've alarmed you unduly—"

Did I detect a smile?

"If I gave you the wrong impression—"

Now there was a delicate snort of irony.

"I have. I've frightened you, I can see that. No need, no need at all. We have a number of possibilities. There are hormone treatments I can prescribe. We should talk about it though. You must let me examine you again."

"Oh no." This was spoken firmly, with utter conviction. At last you looked at me. You turned squarely toward me, your fine black eyebrows drawn together in a delicate frown and anger smoldering in those clear dark eyes, and said, "I don't know what it is you imagine I have, but I can assure you there is *nothing wrong with me.*"

So this was it. You were still denying it, pretending it wasn't happening. Pushing it away, blocking it out. This I could understand. "James," I began—I would have to speak tactfully; I'd have preferred to conduct this interview in my surgery, if you'd only allow it— "let me explain to you something about the pituitary gland."

You shook your head slightly and turned back toward the bar. The disease was progressing, this was clear to me, and for an instant my composure seemed about to desert me—I was fascinated at the sight of you in that uniform, knowing what I did about the body within. Suddenly—it was the strangest thing, nothing like this had ever happened before— suddenly I felt a distinct movement of sexual feeling toward you, a movement of *passion*. I picked up my drink, pushed a hand through my hair, perhaps I even flushed a little, I don't know—such confusion I felt at that moment! I was then aware of some hilarity close behind me and turned to see a pilot mincing across the floor with one hand on his hip, then pausing, glancing over his shoulder, and saying coyly, to the delight of the whole mess—"Care to examine me, doctor?" Spike shrieked—I turned back to the bar, downed my gin and ordered another. Silly boys. I threw a quick oblique glance in your direction. You were moving away from the bar, a drink in your hand, a cigarette between your teeth, a lick of black hair flopping over your forehead, grinning.

A little later, in Elgin, tranquil now, not expansive but tranquil at least, I stood at the window of the top-floor corner room and listened to the thunder of the guns and saw you in my mind's eye at the bar in the mess, a scrap of silver silk knotted about your throat. It was the last time I saw you whole.

The next days passed in a sort of daze. I continued to go about my duties, what duties I still had, and every afternoon went up to the station. Around Griffin Head all the signposts had been taken down, all the street names removed, so as to confuse the Germans when they came. And we needed no reminding that when they did come it was on the south coast that they'd be arriving: Griffin was the front line. The town was a cat's cradle of mines and barbed wire; huge cement cylinders had been put in the roads to block the progress of armed enemy convoys, and sentries were posted everywhere, manning pillboxes; they had two machine guns between the lot of them. The barricades thrown up to block a German advance were pitiful—clumsy jumbles of barrels and tree trunks and old iron bedsteads, and at the crossroads where the coast road met the main road the police had dumped a hundred tons of broken glass, as if for a medieval siege. I told Mrs. Gregor what I thought, and she warned me not to talk too freely; you could be fined, or imprisoned, for spreading "alarm and despondency." One man was heard saying it would be a bloody good thing when the Empire was finished, and got a year in gaol. At Winchester an officer billeted in a rectory was denounced as a spy by the vicar's daughter because he didn't pull the chain after going to the lavatory. The girl said his behavior was "un-English."

Invasion. This is what happens to a community facing invasion. As I sat smoking in my car by the airfield I reflected on what was about to happen to us, what would happen when they arrived. Evening was already coming when I saw you scramble for the seventh or eighth time that day, saw you climbing into the west, into the sun. What place I wondered for us in the Third Reich? I, a cripple, and you—you, a brave sick gallant boy giving your life for a hopeless cause—

This is what I imagine happened. In line astern you ran into them at eighteen thousand feet. Badly outnumbered you turned head-on to them, hauled hard back and swept clear over them in a steep climbing turn and in those seconds they lost the advantage. Your wingman let go a burst of fire at the first one, who sheared off toward you and you knew he was yours. Fierce unwavering concentration, sweat on your brow and knuckles white as you kicked the rudder over to get him at right angles then let go a four-second burst with full deflection—and grim relief as you saw him come through your sights and the tracer hammered home! For a second he seemed to hang motionless, then a jet of red flame shot upward and he spun down into the sea. Then a blur of twisting machines, tracer bullets beading and crackling, the sudden glint on metal of the setting sun. Another went down in a sheet of flame on your right as a Spitfire went by in a half-roll. You were weaving and turning and trying to gain height when you saw another one below you climbing away from the sun so you closed in to three hundred yards and gave him a two-second burst and saw fabric rip off the wing and black smoke pour from the engine but he didn't go down. Angry now you put in another burst and at last saw red flames shoot upward as he spiraled out of sight. And then—a moment's inattention. Why? Sun in your eyes? A flicker of terror? Jab of pain from your shrapnel? Whatever: it was *then* that you felt a terrific explosion, so strong it knocked the stick out of your hand and the whole aircraft shuddered violently. But it didn't start burning so you headed for home.

With what excruciatingly tender care did you nurse that Spitfire back to Griffin Head! What did you think about? Could you think about anything but the job in hand? Did you think about me? The cockpit only burst into flames as you touched down. I was there waiting for you. I was the one who saw you standing on the wing engulfed in flame, then falling, and I the one who reached you first and smothered the flames with my fur. And I who with needle and ampoule killed the pain of a body too badly burned to live. Final irony, yes, I killed you, but I killed you because I loved you. To save you suffering.

And now you lie here in my arms, and I sit stroking this poor charred head, this seared and blistered and stinking black head as they come lumbering toward us through the dusk. Pressed against my chest, mouth open and fighting for breath, and gazing sightlessly up at me—darling boy what have they *done* to you! You couldn't live like this, your face burnt off and seething with infection, all beauty destroyed—

I lift my eyes and look away; my face is streaming tears. Yes here they come, and what is it they're shouting, fool? Fool, yes—fool of love—

Your poor *hands*—like your father you wouldn't wear gloves, and see what's happened to them now, they're clawing. You had such lovely hands, you had your mother's hands—

They've stopped some yards off and stand there strangely spectral in a twilight shimmering with heat from the blazing aeroplane—and what a noise they're making! Fuel, they're shouting—not fool, *fuel*, fuel tank, the fuel tank's going to blow!

Then with a shock of violent exaltation I feel the sudden nearness of her spirit. Again she has entered your body, she has entered this ruined dying body and as passion swells, and Spike howls, I fumble in the black bag with my free hand for the needle. Your black lips parted, a gasp, a sigh, a word. My face down close, what is it you're saying to me? I press my mouth gently to yours and probe for your tongue with my own, probe with tiny darting flickers till I taste in your terrible burnt head the fresh sweet wetness of the living tongue within—